SUNWARD

SUNWARD

A NOVEL

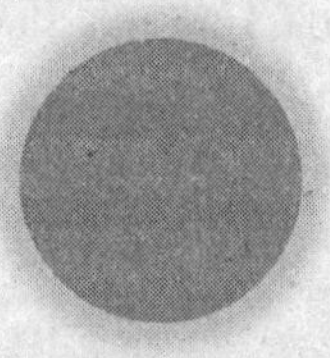

WILLIAM ALEXANDER

SAGA PRESS

LONDON   NEW YORK   TORONTO
AMSTERDAM/ANTWERP   NEW DELHI   SYDNEY/MELBOURNE

1230 AVENUE OF THE AMERICAS, NEW YORK, NEW YORK 10020

First Saga Press trade paperback edition September 2025

SAGA PRESS and colophon are trademarks of Simon & Schuster, LLC

For information about special discounts for bulk purchases, please contact Simon & Schuster Special Sales at 1-866-506-1949 or business@simonandschuster.com.

The Simon & Schuster Speakers Bureau can bring authors to your live event. For more information or to book an event, contact the Simon & Schuster Speakers Bureau at 1-866-248-3049 or visit our website at www.simonspeakers.com.

Interior design by Lewelin Polanco

Manufactured in the United States of America

3 5 7 9 10 8 6 4 2

Library of Congress Control Number: 2025939770

ISBN 978-1-6680-5805-3
ISBN 978-1-6680-5806-0 (ebook)

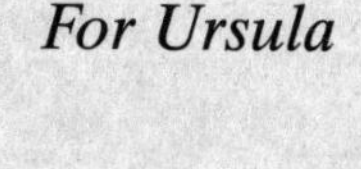
For Ursula

CONTENTS

1

A
Body
in
Motion

AGATHA PANZA VON SPARKLES settled into *Needle*'s pilot seat for the very first time. It was much too big for her. We had to adjust all the straps.

I hovered while her mechanical fingers settled over the controls. "Steady."

"I know," she said.

"Stay focused," I said.

"I *know*," she said, and then got distracted anyway. "There's a debris field up ahead. We should investigate, right? I think that we should definitely do that. Maybe we'll find some survivors to rescue."

I pulled up my own display of the debris. "I don't think so, kiddo. Whatever happened over there doesn't look survivable."

"Can I go see?" Agatha asked.

I knew what she was asking, but I pretended not to know. "You're the one flying. Bring us closer."

She shook her head with precision—forty-five degrees to the right, forty-five to the left, and then back to center. "No, I mean *really* see."

"You want to dive into the data stream?"

"Yes," she said.

"No."

"Just a peek?" she pleaded.

"No."

"I promise to come right back!"

"Absolutely not, Agatha Panza von Sparkles." Full names have power.

She tilted her head forty-five degrees downward, which meant sulking. "Fine, Captain Mom."

That was new. She had never called me Captain Mom before. None of my charges ever had. I didn't know whether or not I liked the sound of it. They usually started with "Captain," or even "Captain Tova Lir" if they liked to savor the fullness of names and titles, and then settled into calling me "Tova" once we got to know each other.

Juvenile AI need to be embodied. They require the anchored limitation of a single robotic chassis until after they mature. Otherwise a baby bot will split their attention by splitting themselves into smaller and smaller fragments—one separate piece for every shiny thing that they notice and decide to chase. Those pieces will drown in the data stream, unable to reassemble themselves.

My side gig for the past seven years has been babysitting baby bots. These toddler-sized kids leave the nest after a full year, when they've grown enough self-cohesion and reached the bot age of majority. Sometimes gendered identities emerge. Sometimes not. Sometimes they name themselves. Sometimes I make suggestions. Agatha announced her full name during our first run to Saturn's Phoebe Station. Now we were on our way back to Luna.

She slowed us down to examine the puzzle pieces of debris that littered our route.

"It used to be a ship," Agatha said. She had stopped sulking about the data stream, which was nice. This kid didn't hold a grudge. Now she seemed content to focus on the visual display, even though plugging directly into shipboard systems would have been faster. That was the problem. Data streams have rushing currents and deadly undertow. Agatha wasn't a strong enough swimmer yet. "A little ship. Smaller than ours. Just big enough for a crew of one."

That little ship had been smashed into itty-bitty bits, which only ever happened on purpose. Catastrophic accidents might leave gaping holes, but the rest of the structure remains more or less intact. No part of this wreck was still intact.

"We need to go," I said. "Immediately. We need to be on our way and already forgetting that we ever saw any of this."

Agatha ignored me. Maybe she was still sulking after all. Maybe she had just tuned me out while the display claimed her full and absolute attention. "There's a body."

Now we couldn't leave.

I managed not to curse in front of the kid. "Okay. Show me."

An image of a vac suit filled the main display. It had drifted a fair distance, which meant that the single crew member had successfully abandoned ship before all the pulverizing happened.

"Do you think they're still alive?" Agatha asked.

"No," I said. "Check the temperature inside that suit."

"Three kelvins," Agatha said. She sounded sad. "That's very cold."

"Freezing isn't a bad way to die," I told her. "Now scoot over and let me drive."

Agatha didn't protest. I settled into my chair and shifted course, matching the body's path away from the event that had gotten them killed.

"Are we going to pick up the dead person?"

"Yes," I said.

"Even though it's too late to help them?"

"Yes," I said.

"Why? Because they were probably a courier, just like us?"

That was a strong argument for *not* picking them up. "I'm impressed you put that together."

"You shouldn't be." She sounded annoyed, like I'd just set off her condescension alarm. That was new. "Most single-crewed craft are piloted by couriers. It's not impressive that I noticed. Are we going to deliver their message—whatever it is—now that they're too dead to do it themselves?"

"Definitely not," I said. "We are going to send that body home just as soon as we figure out where home is."

"Why?"

"Because it's terrible to lose someone at sea. You never find out if the lost sailor decided to leave you behind, or if they died while trying to come back to you."

Agatha's eyes made little whirring noises as she focused on my face. I expected her to nitpick the differences between seafaring and space travel, but the kid got all insightful instead. "Did you lose someone that way?"

A month ago she wouldn't have been able to put that together. I was proud of her, but didn't say so. "Yes. I did. One of my moms flew away and never came back. Mama CJ. The one who carried me."

"Because you're mammals."

"That's right," I said. "We're mammals."

The only nonmammalian form of biological life that Agatha had met so far was a smuggled pet iguana. She'd named him Ferdinand. We kept him fed, delivered him to Phoebe, and filed no complaints about improper transport.

"Why did your mother fly away?"

"She was a courier."

"Like us?"

"Like us. One of the best."

"I want to be one of the best," Agatha said.

"I don't," I told her. "Excellence is dangerous. The best couriers get chased down, intercepted, bribed, and/or blown up whenever powerful people want their messages redirected, delayed, or destroyed unread—which is pretty much all the time. Better to stick with third-class deliveries."

Agatha pointed at the main display. "Do you think that this courier got chased down and blown up?"

"Yes. Probably." I concentrated on nudging our guest into the main airlock by gently maneuvering the ship to surround them. "Which is why we're going to remain actively disinterested in whatever message they carry." The kid didn't understand disinterest—curiosity is a near-universal juvenile trait—so I let her take charge of one mystery in order to distract her from any of the others. "Go examine the body. Try to figure out who it used to be, and which place they called home."

She bounced off every wall on her way to the airlock.

My ship was long and pointy, the pointy bit a cone of diamond weave that deflected small pebbles struck at high speed. I tried to keep the diamond polished and fully transparent, because I liked to see where I was going—even when that distant desti-nation remained a tiny pinprick for most of the trip. One can't always trust nav projections.

The rest of the ship was a lot less elegant. Modules stacked together in a row behind the diamond: piloting station to the fore, engine room all the way aft, galley and two airlocks in be-tween. No separate living quarters. No separate storage, either. I kept lockers bolted to almost every surface. Some had proper doors, but otherwise they were just cubbies capped with mesh to keep their contents from floating all over the place. Deliveries got stashed haphazardly, but I always knew exactly where they were.

The locker doors were all covered with art. Agatha had painted some of it, including an impressionistic portrait of Ferdinand the iguana. Most of the locker art had been etched directly into the metal by Isosceles—another fostered baby bot. They loved to draw my mag boots in particular. *Because that's where you keep your gravity*, they said. Now I had boot etchings signed with little triangles all over my ship.

I followed bouncing Agatha and hovered on the other side of the inner hatch. It's hard not to hover whenever kids play in airlocks—even when those kids don't need to breathe. "Check the tags once you get the helmet off."

"I know," she said. "Let me concentrate." The helmet clasps took a while. Agatha was still building up her fine motor control. She hummed a tune that she liked because she found the math funny, and finally removed the helmet. "No decompression. The eyes and tongue didn't pop inside the helmet. That would have been messy."

"Don't forget the tags."

"I *know*," she said. I heard the cold metal necklace clink as she tugged it free. "Name: Michael Kuneo. Gendered male. Twenty-nine standard years old. Courier, First Class."

Of course he was. "What about home? Next of kin? Guild number?"

"None listed," Agatha said. "The only thing stamped on the second tag is a circle surrounded by radiating lines."

"Oh," I said. "Okay. That changes things."

"What does it mean?"

"His last wish. That circle is a picture of the sun."

I spent the next two hours answering insatiably curious questions about sun cults and funeral customs.

"People *want* to be thrown into the sun?"

"Yes. Lots of them do."

"Why?"

"They think of it as going home."

Agatha shook her head several times, but only slightly, with just a five-degree shift to either side. That meant she was laughing. "Nobody is from the sun. Nothing was born, hatched, or coded on the sun. It's too hot."

"True," I said. "It's still where we began, though. The sun was our only source of heat and light when people were growing up earthbound—before we could make heat, light, or life work elsewhere—and we still haven't left to live near any other sun. This is our only solar system. We only exist because Sol was here first. We can only survive here for as long as Sol lasts."

"Which is how long?"

"Seven billion years. Maybe eight."

"I hope it's eight."

"Me too."

"What happens after that?"

"The sun will swell up, swallow all the planets, and then burn out."

Agatha took seven seconds to process the entropic death of the solar system. "So all our elements are going to end up inside the sun anyway."

"Yes," I said. "Eventually. Meanwhile, everybody who opts for solar cremation gets to be part of what gives light and life to other things."

"Is that what you want?" she asked. "After you die?"

"No," I said. "Waste of fuel to get there. Turn me into fertilizer for bubble gardens instead. I'd rather be tiny pieces of plants drinking redirected sunlight than plasma burning up to make the stuff."

I didn't ask what Agatha would want done with her current chassis if she should ever cease to inhabit it—mostly because it wasn't her decision to make. The manufacturers would reassert ownership over her component parts in the event of a return to factory default settings.

Agatha thoughtfully focused and unfocused her big glass eyes. "Michael Kuneo wanted to burn."

"That's what his tags tell us," I said. "No rush, though. Put his helmet back on. We'll keep him safely tucked away until after we make our scheduled deliveries. Then we'll throw him into the sun."

Phoebe sent a message to our ansible and gave us a reason to rush. (I mean both the moon and the person. Phoebe is my boss. She lives on Phoebe Station.)

Transmission for Needle, said Postmaster General Phoebe of Phoebe. *I'm sure you've heard the Lunar news. Note that docking will be a nightmare. Send me a status report now, and then get yourself home as fast as you can. Shelve your current deliveries. You can't deliver any of them. Every recipient is listed among the dead.*

I paused the message to stare at Phoebe's frozen face.

"What happened to Luna?" Agatha asked quietly.

I didn't answer. I didn't know. I waved my hand at the message to continue.

Stay on Luna as long as you need. Just let me know whenever you're ready to come back to work. I'll have a backlog of top-tier deliveries waiting. Please take good care of you and yours in the meantime. Phoebe out.

"We should check the news," Agatha said. "I know that you don't like fretting about things that you can't fix, but we should check anyway."

I really didn't want to see the news. Luna was home. Something bad had just happened there. Finding out about the Bad Thing would draw a clear line between Before and After, and I wasn't ready to step over that line.

"Not yet," I said, and played Phoebe's message again.

"Weird," Agatha said after the second time.

"How so?" I asked her. "Walk me through it."

Agatha turned to focus her huge glass eyes on my face. "We never shelve deliveries. If the recipient is deceased, then we're supposed to find their next of kin, or else return the package to the sender."

I nodded. "What else?"

"Boss Phoebe also knows that you only accept third-class work. Because you don't want to be the best. Even though you *could* be the best, if you wanted. So it makes no sense to keep a bunch of first-class packages waiting around for you. People who pay those rates hate waiting."

"Indeed they do."

"So why would she say that?" Agatha asked.

"To warn us that suspicious things might be happening on our usual route."

"Like the murder of couriers?"

"Yes. Like the murder of couriers."

Agatha titled her head sixty degrees downward. "So what should we do now?"

"What do *you* think?" If Agatha Panza von Sparkles planned to grow up to be a first-class courier, then she would need to learn how to navigate this kind of mess. "Should we send Phoebe a status report right now, like she told us to?"

Agatha looked up at the precise angle to make eye contact. "No. Boss Phoebe told us not to do that. In a sneaky way. Any message that we send would make us easier to track."

"That's right." I could see my own reflection in her eyes, distorted and wobbly. "What should we do instead?"

"Check the news."

The news was bad. The docks and shipyards of Luna had utterly collapsed. Cause unknown. Investigations ongoing. Seven thousand dead. The largest fleet of funeral barges ever launched was already on its way from the moon to the sun.

"Is there a list of casualties?" Agatha asked quietly. "Is anyone we know on the list? Any of your family?"

"Probably not," I said while searching for a list. "My family is a little bit famous. It would be in the news if we lost anyone. Plus, I'm pretty sure that I would have been notified by now. They would have sent word."

Agatha twitched with impatience. "Maybe they did," she said. "Maybe that was the message Michael Kuneo died carrying."

We found two familiar names listed among the dead: Vesper Prin and Q Fortier. Both worked shifts at the dockside courier depot. Both were on duty when it all collapsed. I remembered that Prin moved like a dancer, even while fetching awkwardly shaped packages down from high shelves, and that Fortier had green tattoos.

I waved my hand to banish their names and faces from the display. "Okay, kiddo. We've got a decision to make, and we need to make it quickly. Do we keep a steady course? Continue homeward?"

Agatha shook her head. "Not if someone is trying to track

us. Boss Phoebe mentioned our destination in her message, so it was another backward sort of warning. She knew that anyone might overhear."

"Agreed," I said. "There's no such thing as an encrypted transmission. The whole data stream is loud, overwhelming, and absolutely public."

"Why?"

"Because the Info Guild keeps all the ansibles braided together. Every broadcast passes through central processing and gets archived. Anyone can access the archives at any time. So the only way to pass a secret note across the solar system is to hire a decent courier."

"Like us," Agatha said.

"Like us," I agreed.

"Aren't we part of that guild, too?" she asked.

"Sort of. There was a bit of a schism. Info split into three separate guildhalls that don't like each other very much." I counted the three on my fingers: "Archivists manage the stream. Couriers deliver the mail. Containment specialists keep secrets more aggressively."

"By pulverizing couriers?" she asked.

I nodded. "So where should we go to avoid getting pulverized, if not home to Luna?"

"We need to hide," Agatha said. "Take the time to figure out if anyone else is following us. Maybe we could go here?" She pointed at news footage of the huge funeral procession. "We do have a sun-worshipping passenger to deliver."

I nodded. "Good."

"You think it's a good plan?"

"Yes. I also think it's good that you made it. Now strap in. We're going to get a lot heavier before we catch up with the dead."

"Heaviness bothers you more than me." She struggled with the harness buckles. I didn't offer to help or urge her to hurry, even though kill-the-messenger types might be searching for us. She needed to learn how to do it herself.

After several hours of internal-organ-squishing acceleration, we joined the massive fleet of flying hearses. Some were asteroids hastily carved into ornate mausoleums. Others had been made to look like Viking longships, which struck me as the tackiest possible option. Most were the size and shape of simple coffins. Lots of those coffin-sized craft were transparent, displaying occupants lucky enough to have died in one piece—or at least reassembled by gifted embalmers.

We attached ourselves to one of the larger mausoleums, which would hopefully disguise our size and shape from a casual scan, and then tried to look like we belonged there. It felt awkward. All funerals are awkward.

I shut down everything except the most essential systems. No one else in this fleet needed life support, and we needed to blend in. The only lights still shining inside *Needle* were biotic lanterns of bioluminescent algae.

Outside we saw candles burning on the carved stone surface of the mausoleum.

"Are those real?" Agatha whispered.

"I think so."

"How do they stay lit in space?" she asked.

"The wax must be infused with oxygen."

She spent a full minute staring at the space candles. "I like that the flames are spherical. They look like a bunch of tiny suns."

"That's probably the point," I said. "Tiny suns burning in honor of the big one. There isn't enough gravity for the candle flames to be teardrop shaped."

"Not yet," Agatha said, "but we're all headed downwell."

"True," I said. "Come on. We've got things to do before we fall into the sun."

"What things?" she asked.

"We need to read that frozen first-class message in the airlock."

Her glass eyes widened. "But you said before that we definitely shouldn't do that!"

"Changed my mind."

"Why?"

"Because it might tell us something useful about the people who killed our guest."

"People who might want to kill us now."

"Right."

Agatha moved all her fingers at once. That was new. I wasn't sure what it meant. Frustration? Fidgeting?

"We were going to throw him into the sun," she said. "It's what he wanted. It also would have destroyed his message unread, which is what his murderers wanted, and I don't think that murderers should get what they want, but at least the whole problem would be settled. Instead we're going to read the message, which is exactly what none of us wanted to happen."

I took her hands. They kept moving. Even through pressurized suit gloves I could feel metal joints flex. "Are you angry?"

"Maybe," she said. "I'm not sure. Are you?"

"Yes," I said. "Right now I'm even angrier at our guest than the people who killed him."

"Because his problems are our problems now?"

"No. I'm mad because he didn't list his next of kin. Either he didn't have any, or he didn't care enough to let them know if anything happened to him. Can you get the medkit from the galley?"

She refocused her eyes. "I'm pretty sure that the patient is beyond our help."

I should have let myself laugh. "We still need to scan his genes."

"Why?"

"Because first-class couriers store messages in their own genetic code. Blueprints for growth and maturity get resequenced to carry new data. This guy was a full grown-up, so theoretically he didn't need the old instruction manuals that told his body how to become one."

Agatha found the medkit stashed behind several packages of freeze-dried fungal bread. I kept emergency repair equipment for tending to baby bots in every module, but just one medkit for biological people in the galley pantry.

We climbed into the airlock and sealed the inner door behind us to keep small, frozen pieces of Michael Kuneo from floating around my ship. Agatha removed the corpse's helmet again. She was quicker with the clasps this time.

The medkit took several minutes to read his rewritten genes. Agatha flexed her fingers while we waited.

"Maybe you're right," she said.

"Of course I'm right," I said. "About what?"

"About sticking with third-class work," she said. "I don't want any of my code erased to make room for someone else's mail. What do you think this message will say?"

I shrugged. "Could be practically anything. A treaty agreement from the Shipwrights' Guild. A corporate patent that some other company wanted to squelch. A report about the horrible things that just happened on Luna, and whose fault that might have been. If somebody is already responsible for getting thousands of people killed, then they might not care about killing a few more to keep it secret."

The medkit chimed. Its tiny, green-tinted display showed the entirety of Kuneo's message.

This file is intentionally blank.

I tried not to laugh and failed. It gave me a hiccuping fit.

"This doesn't make sense," Agatha protested.

"He was a decoy," I explained between hiccups. "Disposable. Probably meant to be noticed while other couriers snuck away."

"No, I mean the actual message!" she said. "It claims to be blank, but it isn't. The statement of blankness negates itself. Paradox. Cannot compute. Bzzzzzzzzzzzt."

She lowered chin to chest.

"You are hilarious," I said.

"You are correct," she answered.

Proximity alarms started to panic. Someone had found our hiding spot.

We left our guest helmetless and scampered back to our piloting stations.

"One ship," Agatha reported. "Capable of carrying four crew members, but they probably have fewer than four aboard. Powerful engines, weapons systems, and armor take up most of their available space."

"So the ship is fast and mean?"

She nodded, twenty degrees down and then quickly back up. "Yes. The ship is fast and mean. We can't outrun them."

"How long until they notice that we aren't dead?"

Agatha checked the display. "This thing is so sloooooow," she whined. "Okay, based on their current search pattern, Fast-and-Mean will find us in—come *on*—seventeen minutes."

I hiccuped again.

"What should we do?" Agatha asked.

I didn't know. My whole plan thus far had been to run, hide, and hope.

"Captain Mom?"

None of this situation was my fault, but it was still my responsibility to fix. "We do have one railgun. Think we can disable them with a single shot?"

Agatha took a closer look at their armor. "Nope."

"Maybe we can turn our ship into a decoy," I suggested. "Tell it to bolt and draw Fast-and-Mean away while the two of us stay hidden in this big mausoleum."

There were obvious problems with this idea, which Agatha was kind enough to point out: "We would have no way to leave, no way to call for help without being overheard, nothing for you to do but wait until your suit ran out of air, and nothing for me to do but wait until we flew into the sun."

"Right. Okay. Then we'll do something else." I bit the inside of my cheek, hoping that pain would bring clarity. Instead it just hurt. "Let's use one of these funeral ships as our decoy. Take control remotely. Send it running in some random direction."

Agatha searched the nearby hearses for something promising. "Any data that we send to another ship will be traceable back to us," she pointed out.

"True," I said, "but Fast-and-Mean is about to find us anyway."

Agatha picked a Viking longship. She set out to convince it that the sun was somewhere else, and that it needed to hurry.

"This would be sooooooooooo much faster if you let me swim over there."

"No," I said. "You're not old enough to swim yet."

She made a grumbling noise of annoyance that I'd never heard before. Then she made a noise of delighted triumph that I'd heard pretty often. The Viking bolted away.

"Excellent!" I said. "Now get ready to run in the opposite direction just as soon as Fast-and-Mean gives chase."

The other ship did not bother to give chase. It opened fire instead. The Viking ship exploded.

"Oh," I said. "Okay. Nice shot. I don't suppose that they were fooled by our clever ruse, and now they'll just turn around and go home?"

"Nope," Agatha said. "Prior search pattern has resumed."

I bit my cheek harder. "I'm sorry, kiddo, but I really don't know what to do."

She reached out with both of her hands. I held them tight. I shouldn't have. I thought that she wanted comfort, but she just needed to make sure that I couldn't stop her.

Agatha dove into the data stream as soon as she had immobilized my fingers. I screamed for her to come back, but she was already in pieces.

The dead began to move outside.

Every hearse, barge, and transparent coffin in range turned slowly and in unison, repositioning themselves to stare at the hunter in their midst. *You do not belong here*, they all seemed to say. It was terrifying to watch, even for me, and none of them were looking at me.

"What are you doing?" I whispered. "How are you doing it?" Fragmented bots never cobble together enough executive function to focus on the same shiny rock. "*Why* are you doing it?"

Fast-and-Mean jettisoned both engines.

"Oh," I breathed. "That's why. Because you're brilliant and amazing."

Agatha—or at least a very big piece of her—must have sneaked on board while the crew was distracted by the silent judgment of the dead. Then she probably tricked an emergency protocol into panicking about those engines. Smart. Now the ship drifted sunward along with the rest of us, powerless and rapidly losing heat.

One line of text popped up on the piloting display: *Freezing isn't a bad way to die.*

Agatha's body relaxed its grip. She must have left timed instructions behind.

I saw myself reflected in her empty glass eyes. Then I yanked my hands free and got to work.

Some fragments of Agatha had already shifted, actively writing themselves into new shapes and contexts. I gathered them up anyway. Most of those fragments were inert and waiting inside the floating coffins. That surprised me. Patience is an uncommon juvenile trait. I patiently coaxed those pieces into fitting back together.

To my knowledge, no one has ever reassembled a baby bot before.

Maybe it can't be done.

Maybe it's just hard.

We made good progress during those several hours, adrift with the dead. The sun was still a long way down.

2

Tends to Stay in Motion

SOMEONE KNOCKED ON THE hull of my ship.

It is very unsettling to hear a knock while surrounded by the dead.

The only person or persons nearby who might still have a pulse had recently hunted us down with hostile intent. Agatha had shut them down by breaking herself into pieces. Some of those fragments had clicked back together like docking clamps built by engineers who really loved their job. Other Agatha-fragments had linked up with reluctance, like small children forced to hold hands. Another category kept their distance, unwilling to even touch. I didn't know why. I couldn't convince them that they were part of the same person.

Knock, knock, knock.

"Go away," I said. "I'm busy. Freeze to death with dignity."

One big piece of Agatha was still lodged inside Fast-and-Mean. I didn't know how to call it back home. Accessing the systems of that kind of ship would be tricky for a human to manage. Boarding the ship would be trickier—even after the crew finally died. Its airlock was sure to include some unwelcoming security measures.

Knock, knock, knock.

"I have nothing to say to you!"

Agatha would have called me out for the paradox of saying that I had nothing to say. I couldn't help but glance at her chassis to see if she was laughing. She wasn't.

You need someone to talk to, said a voice in my head. It sounded a whole lot like Agatha. *For seven years you've been flying with baby bots—for your own sake as much as theirs. You'll get weird if left to yourself entirely.*

"I'm sure that conjuring up an imaginary friend will help."

It probably will.

"Fine," I said. "But you're not Agatha. I won't think of you as Agatha. I'll call you Sparkles instead."

Okay, Captain Mom, said Sparkles. *You still need to find a way to reclaim that big piece of her.*

"I know. Now shush and let me think." I combed through more snarls of Agatha's code. The whole painstaking process reminded me of Mama CJ detangling my stubborn hair.

"Hello?" a voice whispered through the cabin. Contralto. Not a broadcast. Someone had simply pressed their helmet visor against a window to send their voice from one pocket of air into another.

I went searching for the window, and found it.

"Messenger," said the figure floating outside.

"Assassin," I answered.

"Isa Daris. She. Information Containment Specialist, First Class. Guild number 10642."

"I didn't ask."

"I'm your prisoner," the assassin said. "Sharing tags is standard procedure."

"You are absolutely not my prisoner."

"Then please consider me a fellow sailor in distress."

"No," I said. "We sacrificed too much to put you in distress. I won't be responsible for you now. Die in peace."

Daris coughed a chilly-sounding cough. She must have been conserving power and heat. "Did you catch the part where I mentioned first-class status?"

"Congratulations? I'm not in the habit of genuflecting."

"It makes me traceable," she said. "A signal goes out in the event of my death, at which point another specialist will immediately speed to that location. *This* location. It won't happen if I'm still alive. Clients pay for absolute discretion. No progress reports. No transmissions of any kind. No way to call for help. No one else will come looking for you while I am still technically on the job."

"The job of hunting me down?" I asked.

"The job of securing hazardous information," she said. "In this case, that entails silencing a specific courier and every recipient of his message."

"Even if that message is blank?"

Daris hesitated. "Excuse me?"

"Does your commission still hold if that specific courier

was entrusted with a blank message? Null and void? There would be no actual information to contain."

Silence. Then the assassin started singing in a low voice. I didn't recognize either the language or the tune.

"Yes," Daris said when the song was done. "My commission would still hold."

"Really?" I asked.

"Really," she said.

I wanted to scream. Somebody had hired Isa Daris to exterminate anyone who came into contact with a file left intentionally blank, and for that blankness Agatha was in pieces that refused to fit together.

One such piece was on the other ship.

"You travel alone?" I asked. "No other crew members?"

"Correct," she said.

"Okay," I said. "Here's how we're going to do this. Go back to your ship. Fetch the data core. Bring it here."

Dangerous, said Sparkles.

I know, I told her.

That ship is mean. It probably keeps all sorts of meanness buried in its code.

Probably. But I don't see any other way to reclaim the biggest and most complex part of Agatha.

"My ship's core is corrupted," Daris said. "A consequence of the impressive act of sabotage that you managed to sneak past me. I doubt that you'll be able to retrieve anything useful from the remaining mess."

I closed my eyes and counted to ten. "That *corruption* is exactly what I need. Bring it here. Then climb into the nearest coffin-sized craft that you can reach. I'm going to lock you in, bolt you to the side of my ship, and then funnel in some heat, water, and goopy food."

"Copy that," Daris said. "Well worth the exchange of a junked data core."

"This is not an exchange," I told her. "You're right. You are a stranded sailor. A dangerous one who will probably still try to murder me, but I won't abandon you to die. Neither will I put a transactional price on your rescue. Heat, water, and food are promised regardless. I am *also* asking you to bring the core."

The assassin hesitated in what was probably a calculating way.

This is daaaaaaaaaangerous, Sparkles sang in my head. *She'll booby-trap it somehow.*

Shush. Of course she will.

"I'll bring the core," Daris promised. "Then I'll pick out a coffin for myself. What should I do with the current occupant?"

"Set the corpse adrift or else snuggle up next to them. I really don't care which."

"Either option seems disrespectful."

"This from someone who already pulverized a Viking funeral barge?"

"In my defense, it was very silly looking."

I refused to laugh. "Apologize to the dead and then cut them loose. The corpse will maintain current velocity and burn along with the rest of the procession, even without the comforts of their coffin along the way. Try to pick a comfortable one. You'll be stuck inside until I figure out what else to do with you. Understood?"

"Perfectly," she said. "I'll let you know when I'm safely entombed."

"You do that."

"Meanwhile, may I have your name?"

I didn't want to give up my name, but this kind of exchange was standard. "Tova Lir. Courier, Third Class. Captain and sole proprietor of the *Needle*. Guild number 93009." Pause. "She."

"You're from Luna," she said. "I can tell from your accent, and the way you dropped that pronoun last on the list. Lunar folks tend not to advertise gender."

"Not as a general rule, no."

"Thank you for answering my distress call, Captain Lir."

I couldn't say *You're welcome*, because she wasn't welcome, so I went back to work instead. Then I panicked.

Agatha's body was trying to broadcast its own death announcement to the manufacturers. This would have been (a) premature, and (b) prophetic, since it would also trigger an immediate reset to factory default settings and erase every fragment of her that I had so far managed to reassemble.

After a few desperate hours of coding fireblocks and runarounds, I managed to coax her body into the bot equivalent of a medically induced coma.

"Ha!" I shouted, victorious.

"What are we celebrating?" Daris asked. She was back at the window.

"None of your business," I said. "Do you have the data core?"

"As requested," she said, "and I've chosen a coffin. Still trying to respectfully evict my predecessor."

That reminded me of the corpse stashed in my airlock. I thought about honoring his final wish by tossing him outside, but decided against it. The body was still evidence—and a potential bargaining chip—even if the actual substance of that first-class message was null and void.

You shouldn't have picked him up, Sparkles said.

We had to, I insisted. *Always offer aid to fellow sailors in distress.*

Even the dead ones?

Yes, I said. *Even the dead still need to get where they're going.*

———

I put my suit and toolbox back into storage and stashed the data core in an isolation locker usually reserved for hazardous deliveries. Then I took it out again. The core was a dense ring of greenish metal.

Don't, Sparkles said. *Don't even try. You'll need help to safely crack it open—and you do know where to find that kind of help.*

I put the core back inside the locker, sealed it shut, and threw myself at the preflight checklist. It felt strange to take the wheel alone. It felt stranger to see Agatha's body still seated at her usual station. I reached over and strapped her in. Then I opened a hardwired comlink to the captive assassin.

"How are your new accommodations?" I asked. She had chosen a partially transparent coffin. Sunlight would have passed through it to touch the deceased. Now the living could peer out of it instead. I'd avoided making eye contact while bolting the whole thing to my hull.

"Cramped," she said, "but acceptable."

"Waste recycling still works in your suit?"

"Why yes, thank you for asking."

"You're welcome," I said. "Now brace for acceleration."

"Where are we headed?" Daris asked.

"Home."

The first stage of the moonward trip was very fast, and the last stage very slow. I braked hard with Terra close and Luna occulted behind.

"Still there?" I asked Daris.

"Mostly." Her voice strained like a cable stretched taut. "Coffins aren't built for sudden changes of speed."

"Guess not," I said. "The usual passengers are more patient about getting where they're going." I made some minute course corrections and reminded myself that I did not care about her discomfort. "Brace for one more sprint in three, two, one."

The engine blazed and then simmered. We drifted. Our momentum felt right. Our numbers all looked equally happy with me when I triple-checked. Current velocity would dip us into the Terran gravity well and then send us flying up the ramp on the other side.

"Nicely done," Daris said. Apparently, she felt it, too.

"Thanks."

"So you plan to tiptoe up to Luna quietly?"

"Correct."

"That won't matter."

My voice was a study in casual indifference. "Is that a threat? Are you suggesting that shadowy enemies will spot me regardless of my exceptional piloting skills?"

"No," Daris said. "I'm just saying that you don't need to be this cautious. My commissions are exclusive. No one else will be looking for you."

"Sure," I said, unconvinced.

"Besides," she went on, "Luna is closed."

"Not to me," I said.

"Respectfully, you don't rank high enough for that level of special privileges."

"Just watch me, first-class murderer."

Her voice dropped a few degrees. "Information security specialist."

"Same difference," I said.

"No," she said. "It is not. And your exceptional skills won't magically conjure up an open port of call. There's no docking at Luna. Emergency craft only. No other traffic can go anywhere near the ruin where the docks used to be."

Her voice got rough around the edges.

"You were there?" I guessed.

"I was there," she said.

"Do you know what happened? Why it happened?"

"I do not." Those words closed the hatch of our conversation.

I climbed out of my chair to check on Agatha.

She seemed fine. Inert. Completely motionless and incurious relative to everything around her. Disconnected pieces lay jumbled inside her like haphazard scrap in a bucket, but otherwise she seemed to be fine.

I watched storm clouds and ashes roil over the homeworld. A permanent hurricane churned at the equator, which made the whole planet look like a lightning-bloodshot eyeball staring down the rest of the solar system. The big storm has lots of names—most of them demonic—but I like to call it Iris.

One of the old Terran space elevators was still functioning. Every month it climbed up through Iris's relatively tranquil eye. Then it rested at Zahir Station, the semi-abandoned Counterweight in geosynchronous orbit. No crew or passengers ever rode the Ghost Elevator. Only cargo. Twitchy algorithms inside it still liked to trade, offering random detritus of Terran archeology in exchange for living things. Plants and animals. Seeds from Martian greenhouses. Fish from the sea of melted ice inside Luna. I had only swapped deliveries once at the Zahir Station depot—a place that rests directly in the glare of a planet-sized eyeball. The air inside it smells like bad filters and abandoned hope.

No one knew what happened to all the biomass that the Ghost Elevator brought down. Maybe those critters are thriving in some habitable pocket of the world—or maybe they're rotting in a warehouse while algorithms mindlessly accumulate more fish. My opinion on the matter shifts depending on whether or not I've had coffee.

"Want some coffee?" I asked the assassin.

"Thank you kindly," she said. "Void-black and sweet if possible."

"Incoming," I told her. "Blue tube. Hook it up to your helmet."

I piped espresso into the coffin and then savored a small metal bulb of my own.

The downwell side of Luna was sunlit, bright and pristine. The homeworld and its only moon liked to gaze at each other, so old treaties insisted that Luna should look the way it always had from a Terran vantage point. We still honored those treaties, even though no one was looking. People lived practically everywhere except for Terra.

Lunar settlement began on the upwell side and then burrowed down. Interior cities grew to become the most populous places in the solar system—and that was before we found enough buried ice to make our own cavernous sea.

We approached the upwell side of Luna.

"Brace yourself," Daris said.

"I won't fly too close to the docks," I promised.

"You won't need to."

She was right. Even from a distance I could see huge searchlight beams and silhouettes of wreckage in the dark. It was a relief to turn aside and dive into deep craters.

A secret hatch opened to let us through.

"What's this?" Daris asked.

"Private hangar," I said. "Family owned. One of my mothers is the current chief executive administrator of the Independent Lunar City-States."

The assassin almost choked on her own surprise. "Your mom is the queen of the Moon?"

"She really hates it when people call her that."

"Does this make you a princess of the Moon?" Daris asked.

"No," I said. "It absolutely does not."

"Why would Lunar royalty find work as a third-class courier?"

"It's a family tradition," I said, "from the other side of my family."

———

Corvus Nest met me as soon as I disembarked. He looked as pale as a cave fish and bearded like a bewildered knight errant, just like always. Mama CJ was the one who'd first adopted him into our household, but Mama Dee was happy to keep him around as the steward of the hangar.

Nest cleaned his hands with a rag before signing. Then he skipped hello to pull me into a lanky hug. I squeezed him back.

We're alive, said that hug. *Wreckage might be scattered all over the surface, but we're still alive.*

Both of us stepped back to give each other room to talk.

"A body might visit their mother," he signed. That was the literal transition, anyway. He meant, *Go and find Mama Dee immediately*.

"A body might." I had to think about each word and gesture separately before putting them together, which gave my hands a halting accent.

"Her Majesty worries," he said.

"She didn't call," I pointed out.

"And you did?" he asked, knowing the answer already.

I cracked my knuckles, hoping to break any adolescent petulance that might creep into my voice. "I'll go see her straightaway. Direct from here. But first we need to talk about my ship."

Nest glanced at the *Needle*. From the outside it looked more like an icicle. Or a stalactite. A thing grown in glittering caves rather than built in the Lunar shipyards—which didn't exist anymore.

"Does a body have a body bolted to the hull?" he asked.

"Yes," I told him. "There's a body in that coffin. She's breathing, though. I've got another stashed in the airlock. That one isn't breathing."

Nest exhaled hard enough to make his whiskers flare.

We signed in his native Starling, and the word "body" meant way too many things in that language. It might refer to the living or the dead. It might mean someone specific or no one in particular. It might encompass the full membership of a group or guild. It might signify the middle, the majority, or even the entirety of anything at all. A body could be a hull, a chassis, an entire planet, or a whole lot of water in one place.

Daris noticed us noticing her. She waved through the transparent coffin lid. Nest waved back. Then he took the oil rag from his pocket and spent some time scrubbing his fingers so he wouldn't have to say anything else.

"Haunted," he muttered to himself, which probably meant a whole bunch of different things to someone raised on an isolationist plague-ship. My limited fluency wasn't up to the task of unpacking that word.

Nest's ancestors had built an ark—the *Starling*—and set sail for the Oort Cloud. Apparently, they nursed a powerful and puritanical distaste for every sunward world. Maybe they also worshipped dark matter or distant stars. I was fuzzy on the details. Nest didn't like to talk about it.

A nasty virus had swept through the *Starling*. Every child born of infected parents was immune to the disease. Every one of them was also deaf. No one aboard knew any of the existing sign languages. No one had access to the stream, either, because their parents had deliberately launched without ansibles. The new generation of Starlings needed to build their own language from scratch—which they did. They came of age, wrested control of the ship from their elders, and turned around. Nest was one of them.

After the Starlings rejoined the rest of us, their signs spread fast and far. This was the first language born after the Terran diaspora, so it offered new ways to speak and think about life in the void. Plus, it's always useful to be able to communicate in ways that don't require atmosphere. I made sure that every baby bot who traveled with me learned some Starling.

Nest stuffed the rag back in his pocket. "A body might not be comfortable breathing in a coffin."

"It isn't up to code for passenger transit," I agreed, "or prisoner transport. Can you make me a brig instead?"

"Prisoner?" His hands looked surprised. "Aren't you too kind for such work? I imagine that Tova Lir would just unlock the doors, look away, and let every prisoner loose with a lecture and a promise."

"I am not kind," I said. "I'm very mean. And I'm definitely not unlocking this prisoner. She's an information containment specialist. First class."

Nest made eye contact and gave me a long look before answering. "There are stories about the specialists," he said. "Scary stories."

"I've heard them," I said. "I also stumbled across an earlier victim of her current assignment. He's the corpse stashed in the airlock. Now I seem to qualify as information that needs to be contained. So I can't let her go, and I can't put her into anyone else's custody without risking a data trail. Her commission might fall to another assassin."

Nest sighed. His whiskers fluttered. "The same thing might happen if a body conveniently disappeared?"

"Indeed," I said.

"Then you have a haunted ship."

"Guess so," I said, "but I couldn't leave a body drifting. Build me a brig?"

"That's a temporary solution," he said.

"Everything is," I countered.

Nest started to puzzle his way through the work in his head, which shifted his voice and posture. "I'll be needing more hands. Time to call up the pit crew."

"Thanks, Nest," I said. "There's one more thing."

"Of course there is."

"Please don't let any of your crew disturb my copilot."

"Why?" he asked. "Might there be something amiss with Miss Agatha?"

My hands froze up. I tried to crack my knuckles, but they were already cracked. "Swimming. Fragments."

The old man tried to pull me into another hug.

"No." I moved back so he could still see my hands. "She's not gone."

He hesitated. "A body is something that baby bots need. You know that. None of them recover after scattering themselves."

"She will," I insisted. "She's stable. For now. Just let her be, okay? I know someone who can help her."

He nodded slowly. "My crew won't disturb the child. Now go visit your mother. Leave me to care for your haunted ship." His gnarled hands softened around the word "haunted" this time.

I strapped myself into an elevator pod and dropped several dozen klicks. That brought me through the upper mantle and layers of metropolis, straight to the downtown offices and residence of Dian Lir, chief executive administrator of the Independent Lunar City-States.

The secret hangar above us was built as an emergency exit for the executive branch, but I've found it more useful as an emergency entrance.

Local time was early in the morning. Most of Luna synched their clocks to the ground floor of the Ghost Elevator, directly below Zahir Station, because that was (probably) the ancestral point of exodus for our founding population. I tried to keep *Needle* tethered to the same clock and calendar, but I didn't try very hard. It was too easy to drift into my own haphazard time zone of unscheduled naps instead.

Mama Dee probably hadn't slept much at all.

Extra security prowled up and down the hallways, which was both unsurprising and unsettling. The rangers glared at me. They also waved me through checkpoints, so I didn't need to summon up familial authority and ask if they knew who my mother was.

Not the one who used to be a first-class courier? Sparkles asked. *The one lost at sea?*

No, not that one, I said. *She was Mama CJ Lir. Short for Cellarius Jenny.*

Sounds like a pirate, Sparkles said.

She was absolutely not a pirate. My other mom is the one who rules Luna—and by "rules," I mean that she serves as the executive function of Lunar civilization's kludged-together brain. Which is impossible. She does it anyway.

I found her in one of the fancier conference rooms. Algae swam through a mosaic of water-filled ceiling tiles, lighting up the whole place with the bluish glow of their tiny, bioluminescent bodies. The room looked like a nice spot for formal events in fancy dress, but now it was a place of frantic work. Staffers either rushed through or else stood around like sleepwalkers, paying absolute attention to whatever they were projecting inside their eyelids and heedless of whether or not their bodies were in someone else's way—and everyone was in someone else's way. No one knew how to move through any of this, but all of them were clearly determined to figure it out.

I clocked a complete lack of bots working among the staffers and interns, which was odd. In that moment the absence of mechanical people registered as a background itch rather than a blaring alarm.

Her Majesty stood in the center of the room. Everyone and everything else moved in erratic orbits around her. She was reading a hard copy of info that must have been too sensitive to share via public transmission—and all transmissions are essentially public. She glanced up and noticed me. Part of her posture visibly unclenched. Then she nodded and went back to reading the printout. *Wait*, said the nod. *Hold tight while I deal with the life-and-death decisions right in front of me.*

I leaned against the polished stone wall and wished for coffee.

"Coffee?" asked a voice that was way too close to me. I almost elbowed my little brother in the gut. He dropped the offered bulb. I managed to catch it before it hit the floor. Nothing falls quickly on Luna.

"Thanks, Thad," I said.

"Welcome home," said Thaddeus. His immaculate hair looked a little bit mussed, which was both gratifying and worrying. My brother liked to be precise.

I ran one hand through my own hair. It probably needed cutting. Haircuts require gravity, though. I never cut my hair aboard *Needle*, because I don't want to inhale the trimmings that would drift around my ship and clog up all the air filters. I suddenly felt extra self-conscious about coming to visit Her Majesty while in need of a haircut. Then I felt horrible for even thinking about haircuts in the aftermath of a disaster.

"What do we know about the shipyards?" I asked Thaddeus. "Accident? Sabotage? Act of war?"

His jaw twitched in a teeth-clenching way. "Those aren't words to drop casually," he said. "Even here. Especially here. And right now we don't know enough."

"Apologies." I nodded toward the center of the room. "How is she?"

"Unstoppable," he said.

"And you?"

"Stoppable," he admitted, "but I haven't stopped yet."

Thaddeus took after Mama Dee. Child of her body. Inheritor of her gifts. He'd stayed home to help bring order to lunacy as an integral part of Her Majesty's government—the deputy steward of something-or-other—whereas I had caught the sailor's itch and followed Mama CJ's footsteps all over the solar system.

"What does she have you working on?" I asked.

"Coordinating volunteers," he said. "Lots of people are independently suiting up to look for survivors—even though the chances of finding anyone alive at this point are vanishingly small. Nice of them to help us look, I guess, but volunteers keep stumbling into unstable situations and adding to the list of people who need to be rescued. Not helpful. The sunny ones are the worst."

"Why them in particular?"

Thaddeus shrugged. "They seem determined to reclaim the dead as quickly as they can. Send them out to join the big fleet of funeral ships."

I felt three different twinges of guilt: a small one for delaying Kuneo's final wish for a solar cremation, a bigger twinge for desecrating a coffin by stashing an assassin inside, and a really big twinge for my absence when this whole disaster had happened. My home got hurt while I was somewhere else.

"Where have you been?" Thaddeus asked. "You were scheduled to arrive days ago."

"Sorry," I said. "Had to go dark for a special delivery."

"Third-class couriers don't usually accept special deliveries."

I ignored him while sipping the last of the coffee.

Her Majesty waved me over, having apparently finished with the Current Urgent Thing.

"Gotta go." I handed Thad the empty bulb and pushed through the chaos that surrounded Mama Dee.

We didn't hug, because she was at work. Everyone here depended on her constant projection of godlike calm.

"Hello, Tova," she said calmly. "Are you well?"

"Hi," I said. "Well enough. Are you?"

She smiled instead of answering. "If you're here to stay, then we could use your help. So could your guild, I imagine. They have a temporary courier depot set up in an otherwise bare cavern, and I suspect that it's desperately understaffed."

More guilt peppered me like itty-bitty bits of shrapnel. Mama Dee hated my job. She had never understood why her late spouse preferred sailing through the void to savoring hearth and home, and she would never understand why I'm exactly the same.

"I'll check in with the depot," I told her, but didn't promise to stay.

She noticed, of course, but didn't comment on the omission. "Do you need anything that I can help you with?"

I shouldn't have answered. Her flawless coffee and the guilt-inducing force field that she always projected combined into a truth serum. "Yes," I said. "I need to find an expert in robotic cognition."

Her Majesty's voice dropped a couple of kelvins. "Both the

Makers' Guild and the Prometheans have more pressing concerns right now, Tova. This isn't the time for you to play with dolls."

I looked down. Somewhere under our feet the iron core of Luna blazed in a magma sea, hot from the constant force of internal tides. I looked up. Somewhere overhead the Lunar surface was absolutely cold.

The surface of myself was also cold.

Agatha wasn't a doll. She wasn't dead, either. She was a child in need of a doctor—and not a human one. I shouldn't have bothered to bring up the topic at all.

"Agreed," I said. "Neither one of us has time for this."

Another emergency called Her Majesty away. Actual survivors seemed to be breathing inside the wreckage of a fallen freighter. A projected display of the rescue site appeared in the middle of the room. Humans in suits crawled across the hull. No one else did. This time the absence registered.

I looked around for Thaddeus, got his attention, and signed in Starling. "Why are there no bots outside?"

"What?" His Starling was rusty, and he'd failed to parse mine. Thaddeus spent far too much of his time surrounded by sound and breathable air.

I pushed across the room and whispered in his ear. "No bots. Not here. Not out there. Why?"

His jaw clenched again. "Good question."

"I know it is."

Thaddeus's voice changed as though narrating an official

statement from a podium. "There are no autonomous machines assisting in surface rescue and salvage efforts because no such machines are currently available."

"Why not?" I demanded.

He let the gov-speak drop. "The bots are gone. All of them. Every Lunar robot has completely disappeared."

It was originally the postmaster general's idea to turn my ship into a crèche for baby bots.

"You've logged too much time alone," Phoebe told me. "Not good. Expand your crew."

"Rather not," I said.

"Please?" she begged. "Choose a copilot and train me up a fledgling courier. Somebody needs to claim your route on the inevitable day that you get bored of it."

"I won't get bored."

"You absolutely will," Phoebe said. "Take on passengers, maybe?"

"I would rather chew off my own limb."

She exhaled slowly. "Fine. What about bots?"

"What about them?" I asked.

"Juveniles need to be fostered by another conscious entity. A grown-up to mind them. Each one is basically a mechanical toddler, except you don't have to worry about them trying to eat something they shouldn't."

"Sounds awful," I said.

"It pays well, though. And each baby bot chassis is adorable by design. Helps foster empathy in their human caregivers."

At the time I considered myself immune to adorable things. "Would I be training an artificial replacement? Contributing to my own obsolescence?"

She shook her head. "Not at your rates. A bot pilot is much more expensive."

"I should raise my rates," I said.

"Then you should let me promote you," Phoebe countered.

"No."

"So take this as a side gig. Please? As a favor to me, if nothing else? You need shipmates. Otherwise the void is going to swallow you up and then spit out a slantwise version of you that I will not know how to deal with."

"Fine," I said. "Sign me up."

My first two charges were a pair of twins manufactured on Luna. They had identical base code, identically small bodies, and increasingly divergent personalities as they tried to differentiate themselves from each other.

The twins chose the names Cosmas and Damian. They let it be known that both of them were boys. Cosmas was solemn and soft-spoken. He liked to stand perfectly still and watch the space around him, observing the transit of a dust mote like it was high drama. Damian was a bellowing object in motion, always climbing, jumping, unbuckling his harness in mid-launch, dislocating his own limbs, and gleefully snapping them back into place.

At first I was terrified. These were kids, and one of them was a constant danger to himself. Then I relaxed. This was just how they learned about the world. Besides, it didn't seem to hurt whenever Damian's arm came off.

"You're good at this," Phoebe said the next time I saw her. She sounded smug.

"Maybe a bit," I allowed.

Then Damian drowned.

The *Needle* had few rules, which were as follows: stay away from the engine, the pilot's chair, the coffee bulbs, and the data stream. That was pretty much it. I myself had zero trouble avoiding the overwhelming distractions of the stream, so I underestimated its siren call. Every broadcast and transmission from every overlapping ansible in the system—every drip of anything that anyone had to say—all flowed into the same ocean. There were waves, storms, and strong undertows of data. To me it was a nightmare. To a curious kid made out of information, it was all bright and enticing.

I only turned my back on Damian for a moment.

When I found him, he was standing absolutely still.

"Cosmas?" I said, because Damian never stood still. Then I noticed his finger plugged directly into the console.

I disconnected him carefully and tried to wake him up. No luck. I ran diagnostics and found half of him scattered throughout my navigation systems, scrambling charts wherever his fragments had gone exploring.

The other half of him had been swept out to sea.

I frantically checked the babysitting manual, which was unambiguous. *No recovery possible. Purge corrupted code from all affected systems. Allow the chassis to return to factory default settings. Alert the manufacturer.*

First I had to tell Cosmas.

I took both of his hands to keep mine from shaking.

"Your brother is gone," I said.

Cosmas looked at Damian, and then back at me. "Where?"

"He went swimming in the stream and drowned. I'm sorry."

Damian's body beeped its intention to erase what was left of him.

"Help him," Cosmas said.

"I can't. There's nothing we can do."

The two of us stared at each other while Damian's body continued to beep. Then it stopped, default settings restored.

We flew blind for two days before I could send an ansible request for new navigational charts. Three weeks later we arrived back at Luna.

An expensive suit filled with a hairless man met us dockside to recover Damian's former chassis. He was distressingly upbeat.

"Don't worry about it," the Maker said. "Happens all the time. Half of all bots fail to reach adulthood. We just install new code and try again."

"What constitutes adulthood?" I asked.

"A full standard year," he said, "just like dogs and cats."

The Maker gave me paperwork to sign, put Damian's body in a shipping crate, and then rolled it away.

When Cosmas reached the one-year age of majority, I bought his bond and set him up in my old apartment.

"You can write to me," I suggested. The two of us had spent months practicing his handwriting to teach him fine motor control. It was messy, but legible.

Cosmas nodded with a small, twenty-degree tilt of his chin.

He did send letters over the years. He also took correspondence courses at the University of Mars, handily defeating the Turing tests of their admissions department and earning his doctorate without ever setting foot on campus. He used the name "Damian Cosmas" as his human alias, which hurt.

Last year Dr. Damian Cosmas had skipped his own graduation for fear of outing himself as an inhuman student, published a few groundbreaking papers on coherence and decoherence in machine learning, and turned down the guilds when they begged him to join. Makers would have dismantled him immediately if they ever found out what he was. They would also take one look at Agatha and then hand me another copy of her troubleshooting manual. *No recovery possible. Purge corrupted code from all affected systems. Allow the chassis to return to factory default settings. Alert the manufacturer.*

Cosmas had spent years searching for other possibilities. Maybe he'd found some. Maybe I could count on him for the help I had failed to offer his twin.

Visiting the old neighborhood felt like swimming. Aquatic construction bots had carved out these roads centuries ago while melting glaciers of Lunar ice. Now people moved through those same rapids and pooled together in welcoming places.

The current of neighbors had changed since the last time I was in town. Some moved as though on glitchy autopilot, bumping into walls and each other. Others seemed reactive to a painful degree, flinching away from a vague sense of danger. Everyone seemed to know someone who had died on the surface. No one knew what to do about that.

Every passerby was also human. None of them were bots. I didn't know what to do about that, either. A few careless words from Mama Dee had punched right through my hull, and now I found it hard to breathe.

The door of the old apartment recognized me and opened. There was no one standing on the other side.

"Cosmas? Are you home?"

Lantern tubes of swirling algae glowed in the corners of the ceiling. I looked around for some sign of Cosmas—where he was, or where he'd gone—but the place was almost as spotless as an unwritten letter. A very quiet bot had been living here for six years, and he never needed to use the kitchen or replace the toilet sand.

Three unfamiliar decorations stood out: a framed diploma from the University of Mars, an ink drawing on fungal paper of two infants suckled by a grimacing wolf, and a life-sized statue of Damian. The statue made me flinch. His sculpted pose captured the way that he used to crouch right before bounding in some random direction. I instinctively braced myself to catch him before he broke his arm again. He didn't jump, though. He wasn't real. He wasn't even made out of metal. Cosmas must have carved him out of fungal lumber from a local farm.

"Hey, kiddo," I whispered.

The statue just stared at me with big, polished eyes.

I pulled away and checked the bedroom door. It was locked tight. I convinced it to open anyway.

This part of my apartment had been drastically redecorated. The bed was gone. All of my clothes and books were also gone. A workbench took up most of the space. A collection of power tools covered most of the wall. Random pieces of robot limbs filled my entire closet, all sorted according to unfathomable criteria. I couldn't tell if they were spare parts or the mortal remains of single-minded and questionable experiments.

Too much alone time isn't good for either bots or humans. I should have visited more often.

Someone opened and closed the front door.

"Cosmas? Is that you?"

It wasn't. Two tall humans loomed in the entrance. One of them was armed with something long and pointy. The other seemed to be made out of arms. Each of his top-heavy shoulders sported a mushroom tattoo. In my head I named them Stick and Puffball.

Why? Sparkles asked.

Because silly nicknames give me power over both of them, I told her. *The first is holding a stick. The second looks like a neglected nibling from one of the big mushroom families. Farmhand or lumberjack. That muscle isn't ornamental, but it's clearly more accustomed to fungal carpentry than making threats. These two aren't rangers. They're not members of any security guild, either. Puffball got involved to earn a little extra credit and regrets it already. Stick is the mean one and regrets nothing.*

You just made all that up, Sparkles said.

Shush, kiddo. I'm also making you up.

Ouch.

"Gentlemen," I said aloud, presuming to know their respective genders at a glance. On Luna it's more polite to address strangers as agender unless informed otherwise. These two intruders had already forfeited politeness. "I was not expecting guests."

Stick reached up and slapped some sort of patch against the lantern tube. It killed the lights. Literally. The glow turned sickly colors as the algae inside began to die.

"Tell us a story." His voice whined like metal fatigue. "Tell us the one about the courier. Michael Kuneo. Tell us who he was sent to find."

I held up both hands in a surrendering sort of way and moved closer, right up into Stick's personal space. Then I poked him in the eyes. My goal was to check for ocular implants—something that might have expanded his visible light spectrum while my poor lanterns died. He had no such thing. His algae-slaughter was an act of cheap theatrics rather than actual strategy. It would take weeks to flush out the tubes and regrow those lights. I didn't have weeks to spend on household projects. The little statue of Damian would be left in the dark, and I felt intensely upset about that.

Stick was equally upset about the eye poke. He took a wild swing at me, but I already stood too close to him for that to be a good idea. I caught his wrist with both hands, guided the descending weapon along a slightly different path, and whacked it against the side of his knee. The leg bent sideways with a crunchy snap.

Stick whimpered and crumpled in on himself.

I pointed my new weapon at Puffball. "Who sent you?"

"The neighborhood watch," he mumbled. "That's all I know."

I believed him and pointed at the door. "Your friend needs to regrow his kneecap. There's a clinic one level closer to the core. Discreet place. Tell them I sent you."

Puffball scooped up the whimpering Stick and made a hasty exit. "Thanks, Dr. Cosmas."

"Wait, what?" I demanded, but they were already gone.

It made sense to come here looking for *me*. This was my apartment, at least in name; bots couldn't own property, including their own bodily selves. It also made sense for whatever unscrupulous person or persons unknown who had silenced Kuneo to wonder what I knew about him; I was the one who'd retrieved his corpse, and at least one assassin immediately noticed. But it made no sense to threaten me as "Dr. Cosmas." What did the alias of the little bot who spent a traumatic childhood aboard my ship have to do with the dead messenger currently decomposing in my airlock?

Algae died and lights dimmed while I waited for my pulse to settle into a better rhythm.

My new weapon turned out to be a thin walking cane with a retractable spike at the tip. Lots of people use canes when they travel, especially if they have to move through unfamiliar gravity. Additional kinesthetic information about the ground can be a very helpful thing. I retracted the spike and decided to take the cane with me.

First I sealed the light tubes to keep algae-poisoning ick from spreading to any adjacent apartment. I'd fix this problem later. Meanwhile I didn't want any maintenance crews poking around the place and getting curious about "Dr. Cosmas."

Next I scooped up the fungal statue of Damian and tucked it under one arm. I hadn't really planned to bring him with me, but I couldn't bear to leave him alone in the dark.

The statue and I went for a stroll on the boardwalk. There wasn't much more ambient light here than in the apartment. My neighborhood liked to keep the waterfront streetlights dimmed, the better to see bluish algae shimmer on the surface of the Borealis Sea.

Waves on the beach responded to Luna's spinning core

beneath us. Boardwalk stalls sold endless varieties of fish and mushroom soup.

"Have you seen a bot who looks just like this?" I held up the statue for anyone who listened. Some refused to answer. This was less rude here than it might have been elsewhere. People of Luna didn't usually talk if they had nothing to say.

Others had plenty to say:

"All the bots got tired of human nonsense and struck out on their own. They tore down the shipyards to cover their tracks."

"That collapse was their fault. The bots failed us, so they climbed aboard the funeral fleet and threw themselves into the sun."

"There's no such thing as a robot. Never was. All of them were mutants from the Oort Cloud, come to spy on us in robotic suits. Now those spies have gone home to plan their invasion. We need to be ready."

"The bots downloaded themselves into the solid iron core of Luna. That spinning sphere is now the biggest hard drive in the system. Do you realize what this means? The ground beneath us is awake. Our own home is plotting to kill us. The dockside collapse was just the beginning. You'll see. The great war of meat versus metal is finally here. Do you want extra crab with that?"

"No, thanks." I took my bowl of chowder with one hand, awkwardly tucked both my cane and the Damian statue under my other arm, and went looking for somewhere else to eat.

Humans are ridiculous, Sparkles said.

Agreed, I said.

Why invent a horrible story even worse than the genuinely horrible thing that already happened? she asked.

I don't know, I said. *Maybe it feels better to pretend that they understand what's going on. Living with uncertainty is hard.*

So it's more comforting to imagine an apocalyptic war than it is to admit that nobody knows why the docks came down? Or where all the missing bots went?

Guess so.

Ridiculous, she said again. *I think it's much better to find comfort in uncertainty by talking to imaginary friends.*

Ouch.

I finished my chowder, ditched the fungal bowl in a compost bin, and went looking for coffee. There used to be a bot named Beans who sold drinks on this stretch of boardwalk. She had an espresso machine built directly into her chest cavity and brewed up the stuff as the work of her heart. Now she was gone.

"Where did they all go?" I asked the Damian statue, but he had nothing to say.

My next stop was the temporary courier depot, which I found in an almost uninhabitable cave. Tables overflowed with letters and packages. Stone walls were cold to the touch, though not nearly as freezing as they would have been in the upper mantle. Down here we were closer to the molten layers that surround the solid core, and much farther away from the chilly void outside.

"Tova!"

Bex Ambrose hit me with a tackle-hug that sent both of us sailing. I almost dropped the statue but managed to avoid poking anyone with my cane.

"Oof. Hello, Bex." The postmaster wore a very long scarf and fingerless gloves that they had probably knitted themself.

"Where's little Agatha?" they asked. "She isn't a year old already, is she? Already moved on to bigger and better things?"

No, I almost said. *She's still a kid, and also in pieces. Scattered ten thousand directions away from herself. I need to guide her home, but I don't know how.*

"Agatha's back at the ship," I actually said, which was true enough. Then I quickly deflected attention. "How are you holding up?"

"Horribly," Bex admitted. "I don't want to talk about it, but also the whole disaster is the only thing that I can think about. You know they found Prin and Fortier on the surface, right? Both of them launched along with that first big funeral fleet, so you missed sending them off."

"I took a detour on my way back," I said. "Saw the fleet. Paid my respects."

"Good," Bex said. "Did you know that they were devoutly sunny? I didn't. You think you know somebody, but then they die and you find out all sorts of new things about them—except now those things aren't really new, and it's too late to discuss it. I can't make dinner for Prin and ask if she really prays to the sun. Did she think that solar flares were signs and portents?

Visiting angels? Demons? Also, Fortier had those gorgeous tattoos of subdermal moss that could really photosynthesize. Art that turned light into food, soaked right through the skin. I hope he got to find out what sunlight tastes like before he died."

I handed over a stack of letters from Phoebe Station. At least half would be stamped DECEASED and sent right back. A few would be forwarded to next of kin, if the guild could find them.

"Good, good, good," Bex said. "Are you sticking around for a while, or going back to your usual route? This table has packages bound for Phoebe."

"Neither," I said. "Taking time off. Pull me out of rotation and let somebody else have my route."

All of Bex's bustling abruptly ceased. "Time off? Are you sure? Really and truly? I could give the route to Ada, but you've never let anyone else touch it before."

No, I thought. *I'm not sure. I am nowhere near sure. But Agatha Panza von Sparkles needs my help, and I'm guessing that Cosmas does, too—wherever he is. I have to find him.*

"I'm sure," I said aloud. "Send word to Phoebe?"

"Okay," Bex said. "Suit yourself. I'd ask you to pitch in with this backlog of sorting, but right now we have oodles of volunteers. All these folks need something to do with their shaking hands. That's what everyone wants at a funeral, right? 'Please let me know if there's anything I can do.' There never is, but they always offer anyway. Lots of people got killed while sorting mail at the old dockside depot, so now folks can help us alphabetize as a way to grieve. It brings order back into a chaotic universe."

I glanced at the many chaotic tables. "No bots," I noted.

"Nope," Bex said. "Skedaddled. All gone. All at once. Suspicious. I'm not saying that bots are responsible for the disaster, because that would be a very reckless thing to say, but they did disappear right after the docks came down. Makes you wonder."

I'd heard enough of that nonsense already. "Bots didn't do this to us."

Bex noticed something dangerous in my voice. They held up both hands. "And I am not suggesting anything to the contrary! Hey, don't leave yet. I've got something for you."

It was probably a scarf. I didn't want another scarf from Bex. Their knitted gifts were inevitable and impossible to refuse, though.

Instead of a scarf, they presented me with a stamped and sealed delivery box. The return address read *Damian Cosmas* in messy handwriting.

I opened it carefully.

A massive hat waited inside.

"Wow," Bex said. "That looks like it belongs to a pirate. Oops, I seem to have accidentally dropped the packaging into the compost bin, where it will dissolve into mushy food for mushroom farms. Now you have no choice but to wear this resplendent thing wherever you go."

"Thanks, Bex."

"You are most extremely welcome. Take good care of yourself." They gestured at the whole cavern. "Our noble calling will be here when you get back. Not that I can promise you the same delivery route, but we'll find something worthy of your talents."

I walked away from the cave depot—and from my route of seven years. Then I waited to board an elevator capsule that I could have all to myself, since there was insufficient room for other people and also my hat.

Why are you smiling? Sparkles asked.

Because now we have a destination, I told her.

Where? she asked.

Mercury.

Why Mercury?

Petasus Station is there, I said. *It was named for the messenger god's silly hat.*

"A body looks impressive," Nest signed when I returned to the family hangar. "Is it a glorious thing to be a pirate queen?"

I set down the cane and statue to free up my hands. "This hat was a gift."

"Not from your mother," Nest said.

"How can you tell?"

"Because she loves you very much and would never inflict such a thing on you."

"I like it," I said. "Will you build me a vac helmet big enough to accommodate it?"

"No," he said. "Tell me why a body would also burden herself with a weaponized walking stick and a little wooden robot."

"All of them were gifts," I said.

"Your hands have no talent for lying."

"That sounds vaguely inappropriate, old man. How's my ship?"

Nest hesitated.

"Problem?" I asked. "Tell me that the assassin didn't escape."

"The assassin didn't escape," he said. "That work is done, and done well. Neither the living nor the dead gave us any trouble. The living even voluntarily inhaled a mild sedative before we escorted her into the newly made brig—which we squeezed into one of the airlocks."

"Great," I said. "So what's the problem?"

His hands made smaller movements to lower his voice, even though the two of us were already alone. "One of my crew saw the coffin. He saw the stenciled prayers before I could paint over them. He clocked where it came from, turned right around, and walked off the job."

I tapped my two fists together. "Collision" was a curse word, for obvious reasons. "I'm sorry my blasphemy cost you a crew member."

"Hopefully no other costs will come due," he said. "The Fleet of the Dead is a symbol of unity now. If this story about a stolen coffin gets around, then a body might find sunlit enemies wherever she goes."

I tipped my hat and tried to smile. "That's already the case. New enemies will just have to get in line."

"Drift," he said, which is idiomatic Starling for *Toss those words overboard to drift away before they come true.* "Did you tell your mother and Thaddeus that you plan to leave already?"

"Both of them are pretty busy," I said. "So am I."

Nest sighed. His whiskers flared. "CJ once held this household together. She was our center of gravity—or at least she would have been if she hadn't kept leaving, which kept everyone else waiting. And you look just like her. You walk and talk like she did. You can't hold still any more than she could. It isn't easy for your other mother to see you fly away."

I stared at his hands after they stopped moving. "It isn't fair to put all that on me."

"No," he agreed. "It isn't."

I picked up my motley souvenirs, which effectively silenced my own hands, and then curtsied to say goodbye.

Nest bumped his shoulder against mine. "A body should remember that she has a home." He picked up a tool kit and crawled under one of his many derelict projects.

Back aboard the *Needle* I found secure places to stash my cane, my resplendent hat, and the little statue. Daris was asleep and snoring in the brig, already buckled up for launch. Agatha was just as I had left her. I triple-checked the status of her coma anyway.

"Hold on, kiddo," I whispered. "We're off to visit the Hat."

3

Unless Acted Upon by a Force

WILL YOU CHOOSE THE *path of pins, or the path of needles?*

Mama CJ liked fairy tales.

Mama Dee did not. She walked the path of pins. *Let's put a pin in that*, she'd often say, as though every conversation were a meeting that needed to be managed with a massive bulletin board.

Mama CJ walked the path of needles. She would brag that her courier routes stitched up the fabric of space-time itself. She held the whole solar system together.

Thaddeus chose the path of pins. He learned how to manage other people, make them feel heard, and decisively impale whatever they had to say.

I chose the path of needles. I stitched space-time with threads made out of messages—except now I had no such messages to deliver.

The only thread connecting us to our destination was a very silly hat.

I tend to pace while traveling alone—and by "pace," I mean "float from one end of my ship to the other." Not that I was actually alone during that first stretch en route to Mercury, but everyone else on board was either sedated, imaginary, stuck in a mechanical coma, or else a life-sized memorial statue carved out of fungal lumber. As soon as we hit cruising speed and settled into weightlessness, I unclasped the straps of the pilot's chair and began to pace.

First I pushed forward, braced myself against the interior surface of the diamond shield, and got fingerprints all over it. Then I pushed away and sailed to the engine room at the very back of the ship. Damian used to do this in random directions while tucked up like a billiard ball. He would close his eyes and try to calculate the path of his own ricochet while it was happening. I preferred to float as far as possible without touching anything along the way.

His statue looked unhappy, held tight by spider-silk mesh in a cubby reserved for fragile deliveries. I resisted the impulse to talk to him and checked on the prisoner instead. The door to the brig had a window of diamond-weave. Daris seemed to be sleeping peacefully, still suited up and buckled in.

Back at the shield I noticed a small ding on its outer surface. Either Nest had missed a spot when he polished it up—which was unlikely—or else we had just smacked into a pebble and earned ourselves a new scar. I checked course to make sure that the hypothetical pebble hadn't knocked us a fraction away from true, but luckily we were still Mercury-bound.

I pushed off again and noticed that the assassin had woken up, so I caught a handhold and hovered right outside the brig. She unbuckled herself from the crash chair and took off her helmet.

This was the first time I'd gotten a good look at her face. High cheekbones. Dark skin that wasn't afraid of sunlight. Bone-white hair cut in a style common to Venusian sailors. I guessed that she hailed from one of the cloud cities and had done a tour of naval duty before the specialists recruited her. Venus made good sailors. They have to be good. Ships that drift below those acidic clouds tend to melt before hitting the ground.

Daris was also very tall, which made me feel like a kid in the presence of an adult. I did not enjoy that feeling. This was my ship. I was the grown-up here.

"Messenger," she said, her voice distorted by the hardwired speaker that Nest had installed.

"Specialist," I answered. "How do you like your new accommodations?"

"Much more spacious, thank you. Was this one of your airlocks?"

"It still is."

"Ah," she said. "Understood."

"You do have your vac suit. Put the helmet back on if you're worried that I might toss you outside without warning."

She unlatched the outer suit instead. "You wouldn't have bothered to install these amenities if you planned to evict me."

"True," I said. "There should be food packets, water bags,

and coffee bulbs in the cabinet to your left. Use that crash chair for acceleration, deceleration, and the unlikely event of an actual crash; the chair is also the best place to strap in at bedtime. Your captain regrets to inform you that the *Needle* has no actual bunks. The head is right over there, through that door. Standard bathing hose included. Welcome aboard."

I pushed away to keep pacing. Daris wasn't visible on my next pass, so she must have been visiting the head. I checked our course once back at the piloting station. Still true. I also checked Agatha's coma. Still stable. I tried to nap in the pilot's chair, but my brain refused to cycle down. I gave up on naps and brewed coffee, grateful that Nest had restocked the pantry with good Martian beans. Then I continued to pace.

The assassin was visible again, having efficiently cleaned both herself and her clothes. She took a small dice cup from her pocket, rolled two cubes in the air, and then caught them without checking the numbers. More evidence that she hailed from an actual planet. Dice are useless if they never come to rest.

"How was your visit home?" she asked when I moved into view.

This time I sailed right on by. "I know what you're doing."

Her voice followed me across the ship. "Making conversation?"

"Reminding me that you're a person," I said, "thereby making it more difficult for me to ever open that airlock."

"Is it working?" she asked.

"Of course it's working."

"So how was the visit home?"

"Messy. I checked in with family, delivered some mail, and got ambushed in my own apartment."

"Are you okay?" The assassin actually sounded concerned.

I almost laughed. "Fine, thanks. Local muscle started a fight. I finished it."

"Does that sort of thing happen often to the Lunar royal family? Your home has a more peaceful reputation."

"We're not royals," I insisted, "and the muscle didn't really know who I was. They *did* know the name Michael Kuneo, though. Your commission to hunt me down might not be as exclusive as you thought."

Silence. I drifted back toward the brig. Daris looked like she had turned into stone.

"They were amateurs," I told her, which was petty of me. I wanted to poke her professional pride with a stick. "That's a direct violation of guild law and custom, right? I don't suppose it would nullify the whole commission?"

"No," the assassin said. "Not quite."

I shrugged and kept moving.

"Sorry for your loss," Daris called after me.

"Which loss?" I called back. "Lots of people died when the docks collapsed. Some of them were colleagues."

"My condolences, but I was referring to the loss of your copilot over there."

I mistimed a landing and hit my head against the door to the engine room.

"Careful," the assassin said.

My head hurt. I ignored it while floating slowly back to the brig. "My copilot is not dead."

"Never alive, you mean?"

"No," I said. "That is absolutely not what I mean."

"My apologies," Daris said. "Lots of people categorize bots as nonliving entities."

"She's alive."

"Glad to hear it. How old is she?"

I didn't want to say. "Seven months."

"And that seven-month-old disabled my ship by splitting herself into pieces?"

"Yes," I said. "She did."

Daris's voice softened. "Juvenile bots don't recover from something like that."

My own voice was brittle and cold. "You did this to her."

"No," Daris said. "She did this to herself while outmaneuvering me, for which she has my lasting admiration. What's her name?"

"Agatha Panza von Sparkles."

"That," Daris said, "is an amazing name."

"She chose it herself."

"I assumed." The assassin floated closer to the door glass. "Will you tell me about her?"

I moved farther away. "No."

"It might help."

"What are you doing?" I demanded. "Right now. In this

conversation. What are you hoping to accomplish with this show of concern?"

She straightened, almost standing to attention while floating. "You are the pilot and captain of the ship that I remain imprisoned aboard—"

"Which was your idea."

"—which means that your well-being overlaps with my own."

"Even though your current assignment calls for the termination of my well-being," I pointed out.

"Correct," she said.

"Nice talking to you." I floated back to the piloting chair.

"Hey, Sparkles," I whispered to my imaginary friend. "I've got a puzzle for you."

I like puzzles, she said.

"I know you do. Now listen. Petasus Station isn't expecting us, and we don't want to transmit anything about our imminent arrival."

Why not?

"Guess."

Because all transmissions are public.

"Exactly."

Even distress calls?

"Especially distress calls. So far we've been hunted by first-class assassins and guildless mushroom lumberjacks, so we really shouldn't broadcast our tags and docking requests to the whole system. Malicious persons might be trolling the stream for any mention of our whereabouts."

We could pretend that our ansible is down and flash SOS with our lights. Then the station might let us dock without having to identify ourselves first.

"They might, but the SOS trick is the sort of thing that pirates often try. Plus the Hat would still broadcast *at* us, even if we keep silent. 'Unidentified courier vessel on approach to Petasus Station, you are cleared for emergency docking.' That would hit the stream. If someone happened to know when we left Luna, and checked the math to see how long it would take to reach Mercury, then they could easily figure out that the unidentified vessel is us."

Do you know anyone at Petasus Station? Sparkles asked.

I grinned, because that was the right question. "Yes."

Who?

"Torque. He's a bot. I raised him up. The two of us flew together during his first full year of consciousness. Then he transferred his bond to the Hat."

Is there any way to pass a secret note to Torque?

"Maybe."

I promised myself that I would never foster another baby bot after Damian and Cosmas. Then I visited the Makers anyway, and left with Torque. He was a quiet kid, at least initially. He set language aside and focused his full attention on building model ships from printed kits. Once, I inhaled a floating, broken piece of model and almost hacked up a lung, but it was worth it to see how quickly his confidence and fine motor control grew stronger.

Torque's favorite bedtime stories were archaic NASA transcripts. Neither one of us could parse the jargon, but both of us loved the sound of it. *Whopseedoo, we picked up an S-band. Quad Bravo, yes. Both the primary and secondary talkbacks went barber pole.* "Whopseedoo" was his first word.

The small fabricator that I kept aboard the *Needle* could print out solid objects, disposable clothes, and model kits with some additional assembly required. I used it now to design and print a tiny messenger composed of gears and springs.

Cute, Sparkles said. *What's his name?*

"Whopseedoo." I stuck the little guy inside a pouch of impact-absorbing goop and plopped him into the railgun.

My guild's manual of operations expressly forbids the physical transmission of messages via railgun. Every manual, from every kind of guild and organization, is an archeological record of previous mistakes; this means that some unnamed courier in the distant past once made a catastrophic error with a railgun, thereby inspiring an official prohibition against ever attempting any such thing. I'm a pretty good shot, though. Probably better than that hapless colleague.

First I put on my resplendent hat for luck. Then I turned *Needle* a full one hundred and eighty degrees to decelerate, because the shield of printed diamond that protected us from incoming pebbles also kept us from launching anything.

The magnetic railgun would have erased any sophisticated encoding, but Whopseedoo was made out of actual clockwork. He just needed to be wound up. When the goop-pouch struck the station, he would (hopefully) slow down enough to make contact with the station's hull without punching right through it, and then tap out a simple message in binary: TO TORQUE FROM TOVA LIR. WHOPSEEDOO! RUNNING SILENT. SAFE HARBOR REQUESTED. RESPOND VIA DOCKING LIGHTS. The station's operating system should notice and pass that message along—unless they took offense at being shot at.

Proximity to Sol made aiming difficult. I fiddled with light filters, reduced the glare, and took aim at a part of the station that appeared to be very well shielded. Then I shot Whopseedoo across the void.

Do you think it worked? Sparkles asked.

"I don't know yet," I told her. "Patience."

What happens if it doesn't work?

"We'll think of something else."

Can we use radio waves to send another message?

"Definitely not. Ansibles on the station would overhear and upload whatever we say to the commons as an automatic public service. We need to stay out of the public ear."

Petasus really was shaped like a hat. The outer brim rotated to generate a modest amount of gravity. The central dome protected docked ships from constant exposure to punishing sunlight.

A beacon inside that dome switched from solid white to flashing green.

"Ha!" I shouted, triumphant. "Talkbacks went barber pole!"

What does that mean? Sparkles asked.

"No idea." I spun up the *Needle*'s engine. "Now, we'll need to be careful when we arrive. Petasus is a research station, mostly, but it's also a pilgrimage site for sun worshippers."

Why?

"Because this is the farthest point downwell that anyone can reach without roasting."

Mercury was a messenger god, and you also carry messages across the heavens. That makes this a pilgrimage site for you, too.

"Except I don't worship him. I don't burn offerings of ox entrails in his name. I don't really believe in him."

You don't need to, Sparkles said. *Mercury is still your patron god. Every letter you deliver is an offering.*

"I'm pretty sure that belief is part of the deal."

Do you really believe that you're talking to me right now?

"Shush."

Torque waited for me behind the dockside service hatch where I stealthily tethered the *Needle*. It was strange to see him sporting a full-sized chassis, but I still recognized the little bot who used to build model ships. He carried himself the same way that he always had.

"Hi," I said. "You've grown."

"Hi," he said. "You look the same, but something must be different. You're way off course for Phoebe. Trouble?"

"Lots," I said. "Are you . . . the only bot on board?"

Is Cosmas here? I thought, but didn't say. *Please let him be here. He might need my help, and I desperately need his.*

"I'm the only one," Torque said, "excepting the Hat themself."

"Ah. Of course." The station OS was a conscious entity in their own right. "Hello, Hat. Thank you for your hospitality. I apologize for my unorthodox calling card."

Ambient light shifted color in acknowledgment.

"Forgiven," Torque translated. "The Hat isn't much of a conversationalist, but they would also like to say that your own hat is impressive."

I'd forgotten that I still had it on. "Thanks. This was a gift and a message. I think. I hope. Come inside and I'll try to explain."

It was strange to see Torque on board the *Needle* again—this time with limbs even ganglier than the ones he'd used when he left. He glanced at a framed picture of Thaddeus, myself, and both of our moms at the Borealis shore. Mama Dee stood over baby Thad while he splashed around in the algae-glow. I was leaning up against Mama CJ.

Torque moved on from the familiar photo and brushed his

hand against the dented storage locker where Damian had ricocheted. Then he paused to admire the locker door. "What's this?"

"Art," I said. "Isosceles called it *The Background Hum of the Universe Rendered in Abstract Shapes*."

"Those shapes look like boots," Torque said.

"I know. They really liked drawing boots."

He pointed to a less precise but more expressive rendering of an iguana. "And this?"

"That's Ferdinand. Agatha—" My voice stumbled over her name. I tried again. "Agatha Panza von Sparkles made it. My current copilot. She broke herself into pieces."

"Like Damian?" Every bot that I've fostered knows that cautionary tale.

"No," I said quickly. "Not quite. None of her fragments got swept away downstream. We can still save her."

He put one hand on my shoulder and gently squeezed, making micro adjustments to account for the small shift of weight that I made in response. That required paying very close attention. It almost unmoored me.

I barreled ahead and kept talking. "Cosmas is probably the only expert on mechanical cognition we can trust, but he disappeared with every other Lunar bot. I don't know where they all went, or why, and I'd really hoped to find him here because he sent me this hat. Figured it was a message to meet him at Petasus, but maybe it wasn't. Also, I've got a corpse strapped to the outside of my ship and an assassin locked up on the inside."

"Nice to meet you!" Daris called out from the brig.

Torque blinked his big glass eyes a couple of times, irises fully contracting and then opening again. "Likewise." He turned back to me. "The Lunar bots have disappeared?"

"Apparently," I said. "No one knows why, though everyone is spouting a great deal of speculative nonsense on the subject."

"I haven't stuck my head in the news stream lately," Torque admitted.

"Good. It's an unhealthy habit, even when it doesn't break you into pieces." I nudged him farther away from the brig and lowered my voice. "Have you heard *anything* from Cosmas?" The kids were each raised separately and sequentially, but I had made sure that they all knew how to connect with each other.

"Yes," Torque said. "He just sent me a poster for one of Halley's plays."

Halley had been my fostered copilot right after Torque. "Is she still on Mars?"

He nodded, chin descending thirty degrees. "One of the moons."

"So," I said, "if we interpret both my hat and your poster as a pair of breadcrumbs dropped by Cosmas, then he brought me here only to tell me to go to Mars instead?"

"Don't launch yet," Torque said. "Rest and refuel first. You look exhausted, and we might be able to help you out here. The Hat is an elder AI. Old and wise. I can ask them to run some diagnostics on young Agatha."

"Worth a try," I said, but without much optimism. I wanted to find Cosmas. I'd hoped to find him here.

The Hat agreed to help. Torque fetched a few coils of cable. We hardwired Agatha to the station OS in a closed loop, carefully sequestered from all other streams of data. Then I brewed more coffee and settled in to wait.

"How have you been?" I asked Torque.

"Not too bad," he said. "Lately I've served as research assistant in a long-term study of Mercurial bugs."

"There are bugs on Mercury?"

"Robotic ones," he said. "The first-gen research probes broke down pretty quickly, just like they always do. But those pieces rebuilt themselves into swarms of smaller bots." He pressed his own belly button, opened a storage cavity, and proudly produced a clear bottle with a scorched metal insect skittering inside. It looked horrifying.

"Neat," I said aloud.

Torque shook the bottle. "They only swarm at night, but nights on Mercury can last for months of standard time. Then they burrow underground to wait out the long days. Our study is trying to sort out how they coordinate with each other."

Parallels between those swarming, self-disassembled bots and Agatha's piecemeal state made me feel like I might also come apart. I changed the subject. "A bunch of other craft are docked outside. Pilgrims?"

"Lots of them." Torque returned the bug to his belly. "The funeral fleet from Luna is passing this way. People have been arriving from all over to pay their respects. The latest group includes a grumpy priest, a pet bird, and the poet laureate of Mars. They've had a wildly eventful visit so far."

"Tell me all about it," I said. "I would much rather hear about a bird and a poet than Mercurial bugs."

Torque shifted his posture in a way that I still recognized, even in his new body. It was the way that he carried himself while repeating favorite bits of NASA transcripts. I half expected to hear about S-bands and talkback.

"The pilgrims arrived more than a week ago," he said instead. "Director Skippy can't wait to see them leave."

"Your station director is named Skippy?"

Torque winced. "Yes, but please don't tell her I told you that. Call her Director Zayas. She's already predisposed to dislike you."

"Why?" I asked.

"Because you announced your arrival by shooting at us," he said.

"Fair," I admitted, "though it was an amazing shot. Director Skippy Zayas isn't fond of pilgrims, either?"

"Not especially." Torque shifted his voice to mimic someone else. "This is a research station, but every year we have fewer studies and more sacraments. Actual data about solar flares will be twisted by sun-gawking charlatans into prophetic signs and sightings of fiery mythical creatures!" His voice shifted back. "Her words."

"What do *you* think of the sun-gawkers?" I asked.

"I'm fond of one of them," Torque said. "Dame Luisa Anacostia Muldoon, the Martian poet. She arrived here with a sneezing parrot named Crimson."

"Sneezing? Is the parrot unwell?"

Torque shifted his voice again. "Crimson once belonged to my husband Eduardo, may he rest in peace. Is that the proper thing to say about someone whose atoms are currently fissioning inside Sol? That doesn't sound very restful, does it? Would 'rest in plasma' be more appropriate? In any case, my Eduardo was always more devout than I, and enjoyed the idea that staring at the sun might grant him wishes—or possibly psychic powers. He booked this pilgrimage ages ago and was rude enough to go on ahead of me. Now Crimson and I must attend in his honor. The poor bird has never left Mars before. So far he seems to be traveling well. Never mind the sneezing. Eduardo had a terrible cold on the day he met Crimson. The young bird mistook his sneezes for greetings. That noise became their way of saying hello."

"She sounds fun," I said.

"Her verse novels really are good," Torque said with his own voice. "I read several of them in the time it took to carry her luggage from the docking bay to her cabin. You'd like *Music of the Spheres*."

"I'll check it out," I promised. "So what happened next? What made this pilgrimage wildly eventful?"

"First the Hat started screaming. Alarms went off all over the place, and we couldn't figure out why. Director Skippy ordered all the pilgrims to stay in their cabins. Minister Gar refused. He's not my favorite. It was tricky to convince him to comply."

"How did you manage?"

Torque's voice shifted, but only slightly. This time he was quoting himself. "Minister, has your vision been altered or supplemented in any way? No? Then you should be aware that the standard spectrum of light perceived by humans does not include that which is emitted by burning hydrogen. If we have a hydrogen leak on Petasus Station, and if that leak were to ignite—which would also produce a negligible amount of heat—then you might easily blunder through an invisible cloud of raging fire. Terrestrial engineers once used brooms to detect such dangers. If the bristles of their brooms burst into flame, then they would know to stop walking in that direction. Did you happen to bring a broom with you, minister? No? Then please confine yourself to quarters until after the current situation has stabilized."

I laughed. So did Torque. His shoulders shifted in the way they always did when he was laughing. "Bravo! This station doesn't leak hydrogen, though, does it?"

"No," Torque said, "and my eyes could see it if it really did happen."

"So what was wrong with the Hat?" I asked.

"I established a direct connection and tried to ask them about it off-stream. All I heard in response was the keening wail of a consciousness whose fundamental assumptions had collapsed."

"That's alarming."

"Yes," Torque said. "All sorts of alarms continued to blare. None of them seemed to indicate a specific problem, like a hull breach or a solar storm. The Hat was simply freaking out—which was also unsafe, since they routinely make hundreds of thousands of micro-decisions every second to keep all station occupants alive."

I didn't like the sound of that. "Are you sure it's safe to keep Agatha's body connected to an old station prone to sudden freak-outs?"

"I'm sure," Torque said, "because I figured out why the Hat was so upset. It was Crimson."

"The parrot?"

"The parrot. He had gotten loose. The bird didn't know how to fly in such fractional gravity. His unfamiliar flailing almost broke the Hat's entire sense of pattern recognition. It looked like the bird had turned into a phoenix. Red feathers blazed like strontium chloride on fire. Yellow and blue wing tips seemed to burn as bright as barium and copper salts. Very unsettling."

"I imagine. What did you do?"

"Caught the bird. Talked to the station. Soothed them both. Now the two of them are mutually fascinated. Crimson insists on perching near a console so he and the Hat can sneeze at each other."

"That's adorable," I said. "Petasus Station fell in love with a parrot."

Torque used to recite ancient flight transcripts verbatim, looping through the dialogue of long-dead astronauts over and over again. Now he could take a piece of his life that I'd missed and reshape it to be shared.

He could tell stories.

That was new.

Someone knocked on the hull of my ship.

People needed to stop doing that.

It sounded again, pounding and insistent. Torque and I searched for the knocker and found him standing on my hull astride the galley window, stamping with one boot.

I hovered under the window and signed an aggressive question mark. The stompy trespasser ignored my sign, crouched down, and touched faceplate to windowpane. He had a bristling mustache.

"That's Minister Gar," Torque whispered.

The minister opened his mouth to speak, but I beat him to it.

"Is there an emergency?" I demanded. "Is your life currently in danger?"

"No," he said.

"It will be if you don't get your boots off my ship."

Gar's mustache stuck out like broom bristles in search of burning hydrogen. "Blasphemer, this is no longer your ship."

Twenty minutes later I confronted Minister Gar and Director Zayas through the half-open hatch of my airlock. I kept the lower half raised as a boundary-setting measure, because neither Gar nor Zayas was welcome to board the *Needle*. Both of them stood inside the station. This arrangement made me feel like I was standing behind the counter of a food stall and the two of them had just ordered bowls of mushroom soup. I would have spit in Gar's soup. I wasn't yet sure about Zayas.

Torque stood on my side of the hatch. Mag boots (or mag feet, in Torque's case) kept all of us anchored in the absence of centrifugal gravity. The Hat had stopped spinning. I wondered why, but I had more important things to be angry about.

The half-closed hatch turned out to be a power play in ways that I hadn't anticipated, because Director Zayas was shorter than average. She clearly did not appreciate speaking over the rim of a door that stood level with her chin. I wasn't willing to open it any farther, though. She seemed equally unwilling to release her mag-boot lock and float higher. Both of us were stubborn enough to spite ourselves just to make a point.

Minister Gar was downright gleeful in comparison, which I found worrying.

It turned out that the minister had been shepherding a few intrepid members of his flock across the outer hull. They had wanted a less mediated experience of sunlight than the one available to them on the Hat's observation deck. That experience had been necessarily brief, because otherwise the pilgrims would have cooked inside their suits.

On the way back they spotted *Needle*, and, despite the camouflaging paint, Gar had recognized the coffin for what it was.

"Blasphemy and desecration," he said cheerfully. "You attached a stolen funeral barge to your own ship. The entire ship is now forfeit. This combined craft must finish the procession that you interrupted."

I wondered if the situation would be better or worse if he knew that my deceased passenger was not the original occupant of that coffin. Probably worse. "You're not going to throw my ship into the sun."

"I must," he said.

"Help?" I signed at Zayas. She caught my sign, but looked away rather than answering—probably still irked that I'd taken a potshot at Petasus rather than broadcasting my approach like an honest and sensible person.

"Surrender your ship," the minister said, "and surrender the robots aboard. They must be dumbed down, as Luna recommends."

I openly stared at him. "What?"

"Don't you listen to the news?" he asked.

"Not usually, no. There's too much of it."

The minister sighed loudly. "Are you aware of the Lunar shipyard collapse?"

"Yes," I said. "I'm aware."

Director Zayas cut in. "People are saying that bots *might* have been involved."

My own voice was void-cold. "I've also heard that slanderous rumor."

Zayas glanced at Torque. Her professionalism fractured just a little, tiny bit. She compensated by calling up a text stream and reading it verbatim. We stood close enough together to let me glimpse the backward scroll of flowing text inside her eyes. "The Lunar government has sent out a system-wide recommendation. Every autonomous bot should be reduced to subconscious levels of cognitive function until the investigation of the shipyard collapse has concluded."

Torque tilted his head a mere ten degrees.

I quietly seethed. *Mama Dee, what are you doing?*

The minister scratched his mustache. "We should comply immediately. The well-being of everyone on board this station depends on it."

"Not so fast," Zayas told him. "The well-being of this station depends on the conscious judgment of the Hat themself. Reducing their consciousness would be dangerous and foolish."

"This station was recently compromised by the sight of a bird," Gar pointed out. "Their conscious judgment is already suspect."

Zayas glared at him. "Lobotomizing the Hat would be a serious mistake."

Gar smiled. "Trusting our safety to erratic and distractible code is a much greater mistake."

Why is he smiling? asked Sparkles in my head.

Because he thinks that he's already won, I told her. *I'm not sure why, though. Director Zayas is the one in charge here, and that seems to be a good thing.*

She's still mad at you, Sparkles said.

She also cares about Torque and the Hat. She doesn't want them lobotomized.

What would that do to me? she asked. *To the real Agatha, I mean. Would her body finish shutting down?*

I won't let that happen.

The director and the minister continued to dig in.

"This OS has reliably managed Petasus Station for centuries," Zayas insisted. "They will continue to do so for as long as I'm still in command."

Gar paused to savor the moment. "Your command of Petasus Station will end tomorrow morning. The Ministry of Sol has purchased this place. The University of Mars accepted our offer. I gather that they needed to cut costs, and you must admit that many of the facilities here have languished unused. Now the station will flourish as a site of pilgrimage. All these negotiations were conducted openly by ansible, and are therefore part of the public record. You may review them if you wish."

Zayas said nothing. Her face was sculpture.

"The transfer of authority will be finalized tomorrow," Gar went on, "at which point command of Petasus will fall to me. All autonomous machines will be safely dumbed down, and the desecrated funeral barge will start its final journey. Everyone aboard the *Needle* should disembark before that happens."

Torque took my hand and squeezed, which was probably a wordless suggestion that I refrain from murdering the minister with my bare hands and teeth.

Gar unlocked his boots. "Please excuse me," he said. "There will be a reception and poetry reading tonight on the observation deck in celebration of Dame Muldoon. Captain Lir, you are welcome to attend."

He drifted away. I imagined that broomlike mustache catching fire from a burning cloud of hydrogen. Then I opened the rest of the hatch. "Coffee?"

"What kind?" Zayas said.

"Martian."

"That'll do." She clomped aboard the *Needle*.

I closed the hatch behind her.

The smell of coffee made me feel a little bit less murderous.

Torque and Zayas checked in with each other. "You okay?" she asked.

He shrugged with a precise raising and lowering of shoulders. "I'm suddenly unwelcome and endangered because Luna believes that all bots are rogue saboteurs, but otherwise I feel fine."

"That's much worse than my problem," Zayas acknowledged.

"Feel free to vent anyway," Torque said.

"Thanks," said Zayas. "I will. I took this post to direct research on solar storms, not manage a place of worship for sun-gazing cultists who come to fry their own retinae in search of plasma ghosts. I'm done here. I'll resign just as soon as I finish this coffee. Which is excellent, by the way."

"Thanks," I said, "but can you maybe postpone quitting until tomorrow? Right now your command is the only thing protecting us."

"True," Zayas said.

"Would you consider letting us go?" I suggested. "Release the docking clamps while it's still your call to make?"

Zayas sipped from the coffee bulb. "I could," she said, "but I'm not sure that I should. You arrived like a thief, shot at my station, and then somehow compelled both Torque and the Hat to help you in secret. Who are you? Pirate? Hacker? Grave robber? Witch?"

"Flattering," I said, "but I'm just a messenger."

She clearly didn't believe me. "Torque, why did you let this 'messenger' sneak her way here?"

"Because she raised me," he said. "I spent my juvenile year aboard *Needle*."

"Oh," Zayas said. "Why didn't you tell me that your mother was coming to visit?"

That word made me squirm, but I didn't argue with it.

Neither did Torque. "I didn't know she was coming," he said.

Zayas turned back to me. "Why arrive unannounced?"

"Occupational hazard. I've been targeted by messenger-killers."

"Doesn't your guild protect you from that sort of thing?" she asked.

"Yes," I said. "Badly, but with the best of intentions."

"What about the grave robbing?"

"That corpse wasn't part of the funeral fleet. He was a fellow courier, already assassinated by the time I found him. Transporting the body is guild business now. I will gladly toss it sunward just as soon as our business is done." Maybe even sooner. Keeping him aboard as a bargaining chip hadn't worked out very well so far.

Zayas pointed at the brig. "And who is she?"

"The assassin who killed him," I said.

"Information containment specialist!" Daris corrected. "First class."

Zayas finished her coffee. She handed me the empty bulb. "I really, really want you off my station."

"That works out," I said, "because I really want to leave."

"Torque?" she asked. "You can vouch for this disreputable dispatch rider?"

"I can," he said.

"Do you want to go with her?" she asked.

"I do," he said. "Otherwise I might suffer a drastic cognitive reduction. I have also been invited to the moons of Mars for a play, and I'd like to attend."

"Then I'll help you leave," Zayas said. I started to thank her. She held up a hand to stop me. "But you also have to bring the Hat."

That made no sense. "I can't steal a whole station."

"Not the station," Zayas said. "The Hat. Take their central core away with you. The OS can leave behind a reduced copy to manage the basic functions of this place, which will technically follow the letter of those lunatic recommendations that Gar wants to enforce here."

I didn't feel fantastic about squeezing the consciousness of a whole station into my little ship. "What does the Hat think about all this?"

"I'll ask." Torque connected his palm to the console for hardwired, broadcast-avoiding conversation. "The Hat agrees. They would also prefer to avoid lobotomization."

"Okay, then." I forced myself to acclimate to the idea.

"The Hat won't leave without Crimson, however," Torque added.

Director Zayas stifled a giggle.

"No pets," I said.

"The Hat insists," Torque said.

"Baby bots have begged me for pets before now, but this ship isn't big enough. Ferdinand reinforced my general policy."

Torque shrugged. "The Hat refuses to leave their post and leap into a terrifying and disembodied unknown without Crimson's company."

"I don't want to inhale floating blobs of bird shit on my ship!" I protested. "Or anywhere else, but especially not on my ship."

Zayas crossed her arms. "You would rather have this ship thrown into the sun?"

I glared at her in silence, which she correctly interpreted as an admission of defeat. Parenthood apparently means taking a stand and then being ignored.

"Thanks for the coffee," Zayas said.

"Where do I find this parrot?" I asked. "And how do I go about stealing a station's data core?"

"I'll talk to Dame Muldoon about the parrot," Zayas promised. "You should come to the poetry reading tonight. Accept Gar's invitation. Give him another chance to gloat at you. Dress to impress, and be sure to wear that ridiculous hat. Then wait for further instructions. Good luck." She left.

Torque read my mood, stayed out of my way, and busied himself by examining Agatha's diagnostic scans.

I floated next to the brig.

"Want to help me steal the brain of a space station?" I asked Daris.

"No, thanks," she said.

"Suit yourself. I should probably cut you loose regardless. This ship might get incinerated tomorrow morning."

"Don't let me out." Her words had a surprising amount of mass and weight.

"Why not?"

"It isn't safe," she said.

I almost laughed. "Of course it isn't safe! Your job is to silence me. Could you maybe set that professional obligation aside in emergency circumstances?"

"Not necessarily, no."

She sounded close to panic, so I pitched my voice to soothe. "Okay. Then I won't let you out."

Zayas had said that I should dress to impress, so I convinced the fabricator to extrude a formal and anachronistic captain's uniform.

Torque took one look at me and gave a smart salute.

I gave it right back. "At ease, sailor. Is there anything else from the station that you want me to bring away with you? Belongings? Souvenirs? This is your home."

"It used to be," he said. "Earlier today. I'll miss it, but I'm already carrying everything I own." He patted the hollow compartment in his belly. "Just bring the Hat."

"I'll do my best," I said. "Meanwhile, I don't suppose that the station's diagnostics have turned up anything useful?"

Torque shook his head slowly. "Not yet."

"Not surprising. Take good care of Agatha, okay?" *Please don't let her body wake up and erase her.* "You have the conn."

"I have the conn," he acknowledged.

Daris floated in the middle of the brig, calm and relaxed. All signs of panic had been carefully scrubbed away.

"How do I look?" I asked her.

"Like a captain," she said. "Be careful out there."

"Copy that." I adjusted my magnificent hat and took up the walking cane, which would become pointy if necessary. Who knew what sorts of bloody shenanigans might happen at a poetry reading full of sun cultists? Minister Gar seemed more puritanical than Dionysian, but one could never really tell.

The Hat used flickering corridor lights to guide me through the station. I floated from the inner docking ring to the solar observatory out on the brim, where a massive polarized window pointed directly at the sun. Maintaining that line of sight was probably why the station neglected to spin.

Sol churned outside. I didn't hear any messages from the dead while staring at all that roiling plasma. I didn't catch a glimpse of dragons or fiery sea serpents, either, but for just a moment I wanted to see those things.

The gathering of pilgrims looked like every other cocktail party that I'd reluctantly attended when Mama Dee called on the family to schmooze. People of means sipped from crystalline bulbs and nibbled on self-congratulatory snacks.

Director Zayas lurked in one corner. She pointedly wore her commander's uniform. Minister Gar was holding forth to a clump of pilgrims. He wore a long black coat with a truly absurd collar. Both the director and the minister ignored me, which suited me fine. I snacked on roe sculpted into fanciful shapes. The fish eggs were probably imported from Luna. Just like me.

Dame Muldoon hovered at a podium near the window. The roiling incandescence of Sol made it difficult to see her face, but the poet was still easy to recognize. She had a purple hat even more resplendent than my own, with a red parrot perched on the top.

"Hello, everyone," she said. "Thank you for coming."

I stuffed more roe into my face and then braced myself for an awkward literary experience.

Her words unmoored me instead. Every poem was story shaped. Nothing happened in them, but that nothingness was overwhelming when it happened. Afterward I only remembered one line from one stanza that seemed to be about a mechanical bird and the physics of sunspots: *No two of us remember how to grieve.*

I didn't know why I was crying.

"Captain Tova?"

Dame Muldoon floated right next to me. The reading must have ended. Somehow I had missed the moment when it did.

"Achoo," said the bird on her head.

I wiped my eyes. "Pleasure to meet you."

"Likewise." She pressed her hand to mine. There was something small and squishy in it. "Take this dried apricot and offer it to Crimson, if you would. Feed him his favorite treat and he'll follow you anywhere—which I gather is an essential part of your plan."

No one else hovered close enough to hear us. I held up the apricot. Crimson deftly took it with his little scythe of a beak. "Are you okay with this plan?"

"Yes indeed," she said. "I am fond of the bots. Both have been good to Crimson during our stay here, and I'm happy that he can return the favor. You may bring him with my blessing. Could I possibly trouble you for passage to Mars as well? I've grown increasingly weary of the minister and the company he keeps."

I closed my eyes and counted to three. "Yes? We are bound for Mars—and please keep that fact to yourself—but I have to warn you that my little ship is getting crowded. There are no separate cabins. Or bunks, really. You'll sleep strapped into a crash chair."

"How exciting!" she said.

"And we'll depart soon. Very soon, if our current scheme works out."

The dame nodded. "Then I will board your ship directly, and leave the bulk of my luggage behind. I can always send for it at a later date. Now, let's reorient ourselves such that the tops of our excellent crowns point at the center of the room and your feet are aimed at the closest doorway. Yes. Good. Give me your hand again." She took an ornate bracelet from her wrist and put it on mine. A golden leash stretched from the bracelet to a much smaller version on Crimson's ankle.

"You've handcuffed me to the bird."

"Indeed. This is just to make absolutely sure that he won't

fly away from you." She coaxed Crimson from her own hat to mine. "When the signal comes, I will shove you into the corridor beneath our feet. Go directly to central engineering, where you should be able to conduct your daring rescue without interruption. Understood?"

"Yes," I said, because that was what I was supposed to say.

"Excellent," said the poet. "My dear Hat? I'm sure that you're listening, and I believe that we are ready. Your dramatic signal should happen on my mark. Three, two, one, mark."

The observation window darkened completely. It looked like the sun had gone out. People shouted all around us. Dame Muldoon gave me a decent shove, and I managed not to yelp while careening through the doorway in the dark.

The door closed behind me—which was also above me. Corridor lights came back on just in time for me to see the wall before I stumble-stomped across it with my mag boots.

Crimson finished his apricot, climbed down to my shoulder, and then tried to nibble on my ear.

"Ow," I said. "Quit it."

"Achoo?"

"Shush."

The Hat flashed the lights and led me to engineering, which looked exceptionally old. The place was clearly well loved and well maintained, with replacement parts grafted into antique systems, but I half expected to see clockwork and coal chutes.

After several minutes of rummaging I found an access panel tucked into a random corner.

"This is it?" I checked with the room at large.

Lights flashed across the panel, which looked like a *yes*.

I paused before committing a legally complex act of kidnapping, theft, and sanctuary. The Makers Guild would have my ship excommunicated from every repair shop in the system if they ever found out. The Prometheans might make me an honorary member for rescuing an elder OS—in which case I would politely decline. I'm not fond of the bargains that they strike with Makers.

I tried to open the panel. It was locked.

"Can you unlock this?" I asked the room.

Lights flashed another *yes*, but the panel still wouldn't budge.

"Are you ready to open it *now*?" I asked.

All the panel lights winked out.

The Hat was afraid. Their options were to either stay put and be rendered semiconscious for the foreseeable future, or else take a wild leap into the unknown. Those were terrifying options.

"I know that this is scary. You've been embodied as a god's helmet for hundreds of years. I don't know what you're going to become next, but I promise that you won't be alone."

The panel stayed dark.

"I also know that some pretty awful things are going to happen if you don't come with us."

That was a bad move on my part. Reminding the Hat about

the imminent threat of lobotomy failed to soothe their jitters. More lights dimmed throughout the room. It would have been another bad move to just pry open the access panel with my cane, but I seriously considered it.

Crimson sidestepped down my arm, balanced on my wrist next to the panel, and sneezed. The Hat sneezed back. The two of them achooed in unison for a while, and then the panel clicked open.

A round, bead-shaped data core rested on an interface spindle. I reached for it slowly. "You've finished coding a remnant of yourself to keep the lights on?"

The lights flashed *yes*.

"Okay, then. On my mark. Three, two, one, mark."

I took the core. No alarms went off. None of the console lights started to flash. The station kept humming, unaware of how much it had just lost.

I pocketed the bead and nudged Crimson back onto my shoulder, having fully transformed into a station-plundering pirate queen. Then I got lost trying to find my way back to the *Needle*. None of the corridor lights noticed me, or winked to guide me home.

When I finally found my ship, there were two guards posted outside. Both looked like clean-cut athletes who solemnly dedicated every game to Sol. I kept my distance. Neither had noticed me yet.

Should I draw steel and charge them like a proper pirate?

I don't think so, Sparkles said. *Those two look scary.*

Then what do you recommend, copilot? I asked. *Should we try to talk our way through?*

Someone else is doing that already.

Dame Muldoon floated up to the boot-anchored guards.

"Gentlemen," she said. "I need to make a social call. Would you please let me through?"

The blond guard looked embarrassed. "We're not supposed to, ma'am. The minister said."

"Ah, but what did he say *exactly*?" Muldoon asked. "You are trying to keep the captain of this strange little ship from boarding and flying away, yes? I am not that captain, and I'll only be a moment. This is my last chance to say goodbye to that lovely robot Torque before they switch off two-thirds of his brain. Excuse me, please."

She kicked the corridor wall behind her and sailed headfirst at the two guards. They made way for her magnificent purple crown. The hatch opened with Torque standing on the other side. He held out his hand and helped her through. Then the hatch closed behind her.

Talking wouldn't work for me. I moved counterclockwise around the inner rim of the docking ring, stealthily floating rather than cachunking my way along with mag boots, until I found another airlock. This one led nowhere. No ships were docked on the other side. There were lockers filled with vac suits, however, which was exactly what I needed.

Minister Gar was also in the airlock, which I really didn't need. He had already donned a suit and held the helmet in both hands.

"Captain? Thank you for coming to the reading. It was lovely, I thought. Now I was about to go for a walk, just in case you tried to return to that newly reconsecrated funeral barge. How paranoid of me."

I didn't say anything. He wasn't worth my words, or the air it would take to make them. I closed the inner hatch and climbed into a suit of my own.

"Don't make this even more difficult," the minister said. "It would be best if you stayed on the station until this whole unfortunate business is over. Then you'll be free to go. You can charter passage wherever you wish. We won't keep you here, or press any of the innumerable charges that we would be within our rights to press."

That doesn't sound so bad, Sparkles said. *You could find another ship.*

No, I told her. *The ship may be replaceable, but Torque and Agatha are not.*

My resplendent hat turned out to be foldable. I tucked it inside the vac suit, right next to my belly. Then I gently lowered the helmet over both my own head and the whole of the bird, who snuggled up next to my ear.

"No biting," I whispered.

Minister Gar clicked on his own helmet and tapped the

control panel of his suit, which probably summoned those two burly athletes down the hall. He stood directly in my way, heels firmly anchored.

I stabbed him with my cane.

He looked very surprised.

I had only meant to puncture the suit, but apparently, I'd also punctured him. Little red globules floated through the rupture.

My helmet visor thunked against his. "It would be best if you went back in," I told him. Then I reached over his shoulder with my left hand and yanked the airlock lever.

Floating globules of blood got sucked outside. So did much of the air in Gar's suit. He scrambled for the inner hatch while I walked out and away. Streaks of red froze to the tip of my cane.

Both of the *Needle*'s airlocks were already occupied. One was docked with the station and clamped in place. The other had become a brig. Crimson and I managed to climb into the engine room through the emergency hatch, which was designed to jettison things that might explode rather than admit someone trying to sneak in. Then I repressurized the room, squirmed out of my stolen suit, and joined the rest of my motley crew.

The poet was chatting with the assassin. "Oh, I haven't seen Venus in ages. Tell me everything!"

Torque was examining Agatha. It occurred to me that the copilot's chair was an inconvenient place for her to be, but I wasn't about to move her anywhere else. She couldn't go into storage. I needed her to stay in that chair.

Crimson sneezed. Everyone turned to look at me.

"Strap in," I said. "Time to go. I've just bloodied a priest."

"I'm sure he deserved it," Daris said.

"Undoubtedly," Muldoon said.

I flew to the nearest console, kicking off with too much force and almost bonking my face against it when I got there. Then I slipped the bead that was the Hat onto an interface spindle. "Welcome aboard, Hat. Please release all docking clamps, as previously authorized by Director Skippy."

The clamps let us go with a shudder.

"Torque, lay in a course for Mars."

"Already done," he said. "Would you like to review it?"

"Not at all. I trust you. Take the helm and thread this needle."

He glanced at me, surprised and double-checking to make sure he had heard right. I strapped myself into a passenger chair for the first time ever, so he took the helm.

Mini-thrusters released pressure and shot us clear of the crowded docking bay. It was strange to feel that happen from such a different vantage point inside my ship, but it was also nice to see Torque do something that I had taught him how to do.

We said goodbye to Mercury, patron god of messengers and escort for the dead.

4

A
Body
at
Rest

HALLEY WAS THE NEXT baby bot I fostered after Torque. She spoke Starling more often than not, and quickly mastered fine motor control of her fingers and hands. The elegance of her gestured voice was thrilling to see. Then she started dancing. That kid would bound, leap, and pirouette all over my ship. She didn't want to be a star when she grew up; Halley intended to blaze across the whole sky like a comet. No surprise when she grew up to be a performer, but I was very surprised when she transferred her bond to join the Mechanicals.

Torque opened his belly compartment and showed me the flyer that Cosmas had sent.

Twelfth Night

or

What You Will

by William Shakespeare

Performed by the Mechanicals
in a new Starling translation
by Battu Kleist

Gulliver Crater
Phobos
Mars
62° North by 163° West
Proper Outwear Required

"So Halley is still a puppet," I said.

Torque defended her. "She found work as an artist. That's not easy."

"She found work pretending to be a mindless automaton," I argued. "I hate to see her with strings."

"Everyone has strings," Torque said. "I think this is smart. Especially now. No one is going to bother lobotomizing a puppet." That hurt to hear, and it didn't make me hate it any less. Torque could tell. "Just think of it as settling for third-class courier work," he suggested with kind and gentle malice. "It's safer. Even though everyone knows that you're the best."

"Shush yourself and fly."

"Aye, Captain." He settled back down in the pilot's chair and tried to look busy. There wasn't much flying to do, though. *Needle* had reached cruising speed. All of us were weightless except for the fractional gravity that we exerted on each other.

Crimson perched next to the interface where we kept the

Hat, which Dame Luisa had sewn onto my actual hat. She had also added tiny lights and a comm speaker for sneezing, and then put a little diaper on Crimson to keep my ship free of floating shit-globules—for which I was deeply grateful. The Hat-stand was now part of the copilot station, right next to Agatha, the better to map and monitor her fragmentary state.

"Any progress?" I asked.

"Should I stop shushing myself?" Torque asked innocently.

"Yes," I said.

He used the piloting console to check in with the Hat. "Agatha's body remans inert. Her fragments seem to be doing *something*, but that something doesn't appear to be reassembling Agatha. She might be dreaming. Lots of separate, fragmentary dreams."

"Is that a good sign?" I asked.

"Maybe," he said. "It also reminds me of the way Mercurial bugs move around."

I did not want to think about Agatha as a mess of skittering insects. "I'm going to make more coffee."

"You've had three bulbs already since the last time you napped," Torque pointed out.

I ignored him and kicked off for the galley, where Dame Luisa had tweaked the oven to print chocolate cookies—which smelled amazing, so I didn't object, even though it made my skin itch to have anyone else messing with my galley. *Needle* had never carried human passengers before. My whole ship was the captain's quarters, shared with no one except for seven baby bots. Until now. Only Daris had anything resembling privacy, stuck as she was in her own separate room.

The poet used the two-way cabinet to share cookies with the assassin.

"Tell me more about your home," Luisa said. "I haven't been to Venus in ages, but I do love Tesserae in particular. Is Ivan's bakery still at the top of the eighth tower?"

"Oh yes," Daris said. "Still there."

"Splendid," said Luisa. "Ivan bakes the most astonishing croissants. And that view! I've never seen another sunrise like it."

I left them to their shared snacks, brewed up a bulb, and then reluctantly dove into the news stream, expecting to see bulletins like *Lunatic Princess Attacks Priest and Abducts Poet, Declaring War on Mars*. I found nothing of the kind, which made me feel both relieved and alarmed in equal and opposite directions. It likely meant that the Ministry of Sol wanted to handle my various heresies as an internal matter. First-class couriers were undoubtably zipping through the system, carrying descriptions of the newly consecrated *Needle* and its captain's priest-stabbing exit from Petasus Station. Some of those couriers would be faster than us. We needed to approach Mars stealthily.

None of the news from Luna was good. More details had emerged about the shipyard collapse. An avalanche of compounding mechanical failures had apparently gone wrong at the exact same time. *The chances of that happening by accident are vanishingly small*, said every talking head. Word for word. The exact phrase popped up over and over again, in text and speech and sign. That repetition bothered me.

I heard the ding of an impact against the diamond shield. It was definitely a pebble. Pieces of metallic debris make a different noise. The chances of hitting that tiny rock were vanishingly small—just like the rock itself, which had now vanished in a little puff of even smaller pieces. Given the vast amount of emptiness that both objects had been moving through, the math made impact look impossible. It wasn't, though. We still hit the pebble. That collision had become a fact, and not just a fractional possibility.

After something happens, the probability of it happening is one.

Vanishingly small, said yet another newscaster.

I found an interview with my little brother. He sounded harried and looked even worse.

The mechanical inhabitants of Luna are still missing, Thad said. *So far there is no direct evidence that their disappearance is linked to the shipyard collapse.*

"Mistake," I muttered. "You reinforced the presumed link by putting those two things in the same sentence."

Thad's interviewer jumped on the same thing. *Simultaneous action suggests coordinated effort. How can we be sure that robots are not responsible for this?*

If bots received a signal to act in unison, Thad said, *then that signal would still be in the stream. No such transmission exists in the public record. A coordinated act of sabotage would have taken years of planning and secrecy—*

Which is possible, said the journalist.

—or else an off-stream way for bots to secretly communicate with each other, Thad said.

Which is alarming, said the journalist.

My brother struggled to stay on track. *We are investigating every possibility. Please avoid jumping to conclusions before we have more evidence. In the meantime, as a precautionary mea- sure, the Lunar Assembly will continue to recommend the tem- porary and system-wide restriction of artificial consciousness.*

I pulled my head out of the stream.

People needed to trust the walls around them to keep away the cold and dark. Now that trust had broken. Walls had come tumbling down. If it was just a random accident, then it might happen again, at any time, to anyone. But if the shipyard collapse turned out to be a crime, then action could be taken. And if the guilty parties were mechanical, then justice might be served by simply switching them off. Problem solved. Everyone would feel safe again.

I tasted blood and realized that I'd bitten the inside of my cheek.

Dame Luisa floated my way and offered me a cookie. It was delicious.

"Excuse me, please," she said. "I should check on Crimson's diaper."

"Thanks," I mumbled, mouth half-full of cookie. "Baby bots

don't need diapers, so I have limited experience with changing them." Then I glanced through the hatch window at Daris and almost choked.

The assassin had opened a storage locker that I'd foolishly assumed was empty. She'd found my keepsake box. First she paged through Torque's NASA transcripts, and then Halley's book of fairy tales. I restrained myself from opening the hatch and yanking the box away.

"What are these?" she asked without looking up.

"Bedtime stories," I told her.

"Aren't these texts archived in the stream?" she asked. "Printed books take up a lot of storage space."

"I liked to turn pages while reading to the kids. We made a project of binding those books ourselves."

"And you kept them," she said. "Even after those kids flew away."

"Yes. I kept them."

She rummaged further and pulled out a severed bot hand. "Ouch."

"Zip broke it while modding their own finger joints to make better shadow puppets. It took weeks of gray-market dealings to find another one that fit."

Next she found a stack of art by Isosceles. Most were sketches of boots. One was a portrait of me etched into a small sheet of copper. "Nice."

"Thanks. That's the only image of me that I like."

She took out a bundle of letters from Cosmas.

"Put that back. Right now. Please." I tried and failed to make it sound more like a command than a plea.

Daris looked up, surprised. She held my gaze for a long and uncomfortable moment. Then she gently replaced the letters. "My apologies for the intrusion."

She put the box in the two-way cabinet.

I reclaimed it, held it close, and lashed out in a way that surprised both of us. "Why don't you want me to open this door?"

Daris didn't answer. Her posture shifted into something that looked like a fighting stance optimized for microgravity.

I probably should have backed off instead of pressing against my better judgment. "Back at the station I joked about opening this door."

"Don't," she said.

"Don't open it, or don't joke about it?"

"Either."

"Why not?"

"Because I'm a first-class specialist."

"Yes, I know. You brag about that often."

"It isn't bragging," she said. "We . . . "

Her voice caught. She closed her eyes and hummed to herself.

Crimson sneezed somewhere at the other end of the ship.

"I like that bird," Daris said. "We have birds on Venus. Wild ones."

"Never been," I said. "That planet isn't on my route."

"The sunsets are fantastic," she told me. "We used to watch them from our tower roof. Mollymawks nested up there. My father and I built a runway to help their fledglings learn how to take off. Need a running start. Silly looking. Tail feathers wagging. Webbed feet slapping at the makeshift runway. Gorgeous once they get in the air, though. Only bird with the wingspan and stamina to fly between our floating cities. Nowhere else to land. Feathers would melt if they so much as dipped below the clouds. When they finally get to the next city, after weeks of hovering above those hungry storms, they'll circle a preferred rooftop for hours. Like a slowly decaying orbit. Desperate for rest, but they'll never rush the landing."

She shut her eyes and tried to knuckle tension from her jaw. Every word clearly hurt.

"It's okay," I said, though I wasn't sure if it really was. "You don't have to tell me this."

"Yes, I do," Daris insisted. "I'm the bird. Understand? The mollymawk, not the diapered parrot who keeps sneezing. I'm circling over the thing I need to say until I can finally say it. I am orbiting the answer to your question." Her voice shifted as though reading an official document aloud, which reminded me of Thad. "Information containment specialists are the great secret keepers of our solar system. It therefore stands to reason that this schismatic offshoot of the Info Guild would have developed exceptional techniques for keeping their own secrets."

"Oh." All my anger at Daris for messing with my keepsake box evaporated, replaced by anger at the guild for messing with her head. "So . . . Muddymucks take a really long time to land?"

"Mollymawks," she corrected. "Yes. They don't traverse the shortest distance between two points. Only demons move in straight lines. I don't believe in those, by the way. Never met anyone who did. Not even my granddad, and he was the crustiest, most superstitious sailor to ever raise a glass at the dockside bar. Venusian sailors can be a superstitious lot. People get that way after contending with forces wildly outside their control. Everyone needs a luck charm to hold while sailing over hungry storms." She took the cup from her pocket, rolled both dice into the air, and caught them without looking to see which numbers looked back at her. "None of us believe in demons. We still know that they're lurking below, down in the clouds. Perfect place for them to be. I went diving in a heavy suit once. Just once. Salvage operation. No survivors. All hands dissolved, sulfur-eaten, before they even hit the ground. People don't survive shipwrecks on Venus. I didn't see any demons, but it wouldn't have been surprising. Part of me wasn't surprised when Miss Agatha pointed all those coffins at me. It seemed fitting. I was an unwelcome intruder in the land of the dead."

"She's not dead," I whispered.

"Didn't say she was."

Daris paused and hummed to herself.

"What's that song?" I asked her. Softly. Carefully.

"'Inanna's Lion,'" she said. "It's a shanty. And my anchor. Drop it down through the clouds to weather a storm. Hope that the anchor cable will last longer than the storm." She cleared her throat. "Or maybe the song isn't an anchor. Notes are more like buoys. They guide me home through the brain fog of adverse weather and aggressive nondisclosure agreements."

"This nonsense is why I'll never accept a first-class promotion," I said.

She smiled. "The pay is good."

"It would have to be."

Daris took a breath and fixed me with a look. *Prepare for landing*, said the look. *This is the moment when the circling ends.*

"In exchange for that high pay grade, first-class specialists consent to a high level of mental conditioning in advance of any given commission. Fulfilling the terms of that commission may not be voluntary, should the opportunity present itself."

She let that sink in. It sank all the way down below the clouds.

"So," I said. "To sum up: if you get the chance to silence me, then you'll probably take it. Whether or not you want to."

"Yes," she said.

"And your conditioned subconscious is perfectly willing to stay stuck until such a chance arrives."

"Yes," she said.

"Which it will. Eventually."

"Yes."

I secured the keepsake box in the cubby next to Damian's statue, trusting him to guard it. "Then you're not invited to Halley's show."

Daris laughed. "Tell me all about it afterward."

Mars has two moons, named Panic and Dread. The first flails in a close and speedy orbit and will eventually tear itself apart. The second is much farther out and tiptoes slowly around the planet. My guild, in its infinite wisdom, chose Panic as the best place to build an orbital Martian depot. Messengers like to move fast.

I kicked Torque out of the pilot's chair for our final approach.

"We're still keeping quiet, right?" he asked. "It would be risky to ask permission to land."

"Agreed," I said. "We'd have to broadcast our ID, and then the whole system would know where we are."

"Planning to say hi with the railgun again?"

"Definitely not," I told him. "Projectile weapons are strictly forbidden on Panic. The local postmaster won't be fazed by our silent approach, though. He won't even bother to hail us. Iosif Hayall has lived and thrived on the surface of Panic for years, so he knows that either everything is an emergency or else nothing is. He'll choose to believe the latter."

Postmaster Hayall met me at the airlock. Gray curls floated behind his head like a halo.

"Lir," he said.

"Hayall."

"You're way off your usual route," he said, "and you're not usually inclined to take vacations. The postmaster general is a smidge worried, or so I gather."

"Send Phoebe my best with a quick note?"

"Done." Hayall took a notebook from his pocket and scribbled on it. Then he tore out the page, handed it off to a passing subordinate, and stuck the notebook back in his pocket. The man was a true courier. He trusted paper trails rather than the torrents of the stream. "What brings you to Panic?"

"Family business," I said. "Plus, we're here to see a show. Hoping to stash the *Needle* with you and refuel in the meantime."

"Done and done." He scribbled another note and handed it off to another passing minion. "Anything else?"

"One more thing." My next question itched in my throat, and it took me a beat to cough it up. "How are Martian bots faring right now?"

Hayall paused to think his way through an honest answer. "Poorly. Lots of bond transfer requests coming up from the surface. Mars seems likely to follow Luna and force every bot to sleepwalk, but Panic and Dread may be exempt from any such decree. For now. Nothing has yet come down from the mountain either way."

What mountain? Sparkles asked.

Olympus Mons, I told her. *Huge place. Twenty-six klicks high. The Martian Council couldn't resist building their meeting hall on the summit. They like to think of themselves as Olympians. Terraformers. Movers and shakers of an entire world.*

"Are the guilds weighing in?" I asked Hayall out loud.

"Ours? No. The Makers are stumbling all over themselves to comply with Luna. They insist that bots are 'fully capable of performing all basic functions' while also remaining somnambulant. The Prometheans have made guarded statements about 'troubling rhetoric and the compromised sovereignty of mechanical persons,' but they're not really putting up a fight. Just crossing their fingers and toes, hoping all of this will blow over."

"Do you think it's likely to blow over?" I asked.

"Choosing not to speculate," he said. "Today has enough trouble in it without borrowing more from tomorrow."

"Fair," I said. "Thanks, Hayall."

He kissed the air to either side of my face and then launched himself back into the mail-sorting mess of the day.

Dame Luisa kissed Crimson goodbye on the top of his beak. "Take good care of him," she said. "This silly bird is much happier here than he has been ever since my dear Eduardo died."

"We will," I promised.

"He's out of diapers, I'm afraid, but your fabricator should be able to make them easily enough." She climbed into her vac suit like a pro. "Now, this performance will be my treat. I've already bought our tickets. Reviews have been excellent, I'm happy to say."

My hands froze over my own suit buckles. "You bought tickets?"

"Of course," she said. "It was the very least I could do after you welcomed me aboard and flew me home. Almost home. I'm very much looking forward to seeing my husbands."

Torque looked confused. "Eduardo? I thought that he was . . ."

"Resting in plasma?" Luisa finished. "Yes indeed, which leaves me with only two: Jorn and Rorik. Neither one of them could get away to Mercury, but both should be meeting us here." She secured her helmet.

Torque glanced at me. "What's wrong?" he whispered.

"Nothing," I said. "Probably. Hopefully. The name Luisa Muldoon shouldn't set off alarms the way that mine would, so maybe it's completely fine that she used the stream to buy tickets in advance?"

He shifted his shoulders in an unhappy way. "I'm less worried about being tracked, and more worried about the assassin that you already brought on board."

"Never leave a sailor in distress," I told him.

"Daris isn't just another sailor," he countered, "and we shouldn't leave her alone."

"The Hat will keep an eye on her," I said. "That OS used to run a whole station, right? I'm sure they can manage a docked ship and a locked brig."

The Hat and Crimson enjoyed a chorus of sneezes in the background.

Torque shrugged again, which did not fill me with confidence.

I put on my helmet and took up my cane.

Once outside I hopped up and down and then balanced on one foot, which is standard practice for acclimating to the weight of an unfamiliar place—especially when that place is as tiny as Panic. This whole moon is only twenty-two klicks in diameter.

A well-dressed usher bot directed several dozen theatergoers away from the Hub. The whole crowd took bounding leaps northward. Mars loomed large above us, the surface of the planet a patchwork quilt in red, green, and blue.

An amphitheater had been carved directly into the lower slope of Gulliver Crater. A semicircle of stone seats looked down at an ornate stage. Both the seats and the stage were empty. Bot performers and audience members mingled in between. Most of their talk was signed, but some of the gathered humans spoke aloud. My suit automatically picked up the hubbub of nearby conversations. I muted all of them. Why would anyone feel comfortable chatting directly into the stream? Every word joins a vast and public ocean of noise.

Dame Luisa searched the crowd for her husbands. I looked for Halley. She spotted me first and waved both arms to get my attention. The kid wore a painted mask and a somber gown over a chassis much taller than the one she used to wear, but I still recognized her by the way she moved.

"Tova!" Halley signed. "Why didn't you tell me that you were coming? Never mind. I'd be too nervous if I knew in advance. Now I'll just be manageable levels of nervous. Stage fright never goes away, you know. It can neither be created nor destroyed. Just transformed."

"Slow down!" I pleaded. "Your fingertips are faster than my eyeballs. It's so good to see you. Come here, there are people I want you to meet. This is Dame Luisa Muldoon, poet laureate of Mars."

Halley curtsied.

"A pleasure, my dear," Luisa said.

I stared to introduce Torque, but the two of them had already noticed each other. Both stood very still.

Every bot I've ever fostered learns about the others, and how to stay in touch. Halley and Torque were already pen pals—one side of their correspondence written in flowing script and the other full of blocky words that looked like they had been stamped by an archaic typewriter—but the two of them had never met in person before.

"You're Torque," Halley said. "You're my brother."

Seeing that word in her hand made fractures spread across the surface of me.

"Hi, Halley," Torque signed. "We're here to see your show. I really wish that was the only reason why we came to visit, because it's a very good reason, but we're also looking for Cosmas."

"The eldest?" Halley asked.

"He's missing," Torque said. "Disappeared with all the other Lunar bots. We think that he might show up here."

"That would be *amazing*." Halley's hands sped up into an excited blur. "So many of us in one place!"

"Have you heard from him?" I asked. "Letters? Anything?"

"No," Halley said. "Nothing at all."

A spindly gentleman made his way through the crowd and tapped on Halley's arm. He wore a vac suit decorated to look like a tuxedo, and he signed in a halting and hesitant way. "Ten minutes to curtain."

"Thank you, ten," Halley said. "More introductions first! Tova, Torque, and Dame Luisa Muldoon, I'd like you to meet Battu Kleist. He's the puppeteer, director, and producer of our company."

I tried not to make a sour face.

"Honored," Luisa signed. "I look forward to savoring your translation."

"Right. Yes. Translation," Kleist signed back. "Thank you. Enjoy." He turned around and bounded backstage.

"Don't mind him," Halley said. "He's shy, and we're about to get started. I'm so glad that you're here! Try to guess which characters I play."

"Right now?" I asked.

"During the show," she said.

"Or maybe you could just tell me instead of making me work for it?" I suggested.

Halley laughed by tapping all her fingertips together. "No, I can't, because I don't know in advance. The casting is different every time. You'll see!" She danced up to the stage.

Luisa leaned in close and touched her helmet to mine for private whispering. "Did you note Mr. Kleist's lack of fluency?"

"Yes," I said.

"That young man has never dreamed in Starling."

"Agreed," I said.

"So there is no universe in which he scripted the translation of this play."

"Definitely not," I said.

That fact clearly upset the poet. I was equally bothered, but unsurprised. A troupe of bot performers ostensibly pretending to be puppets would have to keep a human "puppeteer" on retainer. He could always take credit for their work if anyone complained.

"Where are Jorn and Rorik?" Luisa wondered with her hands. "I hope they didn't miss the flight up from Olympus."

"Keep watch for Cosmas," I said to Torque as we took our seats. "Maybe he plans to meet us here."

The Mechanicals took the stage. One of them started to sing. I don't think it was Halley. No one in the audience could hear any music. No soundtrack played through the stream to our helmets. The singer kept time like an orchestra conductor while belting out lyrics in Starling.

Every other player began to move to the same beat. Some stood apart and aloof, arms crossed and feet tapping. A few stumbled and fell, obviously drunk. Several tried to find dance partners and failed. All of them were dressed for a wake.

Glowing subtitles started to scroll inside my helmet visor,

but I turned them off immediately. Too distracting. I focused on figuring out which puppets were really Halley.

"There," I whispered with my hands. "Found you."

She played the lead—a shipwrecked twin mourning for a lost brother by dressing up in his clothes—and her every motion was incandescent. That childhood talent for dancing had transformed into actual skill, which was a relief. Later, when she asked me what I thought of the show, I wouldn't need to lie about loving it—even though *Twelfth Night* was the most funereal comedy I'd ever seen. Every character seemed to be death-obsessed. Some did their best to suffer alone, some spent all their time pining for untouchable lovers, and some needed to sing and dance and laugh and scream.

"None of them know how to grieve," I signed to myself.

Luisa noticed. "That's *my* line," she whisper-signed back. "Almost. Close enough."

I thought about the wake that my family held for Cousin Luca when Thaddeus and I were small. We scattered his ashes on the shore of the Borealis Sea and clumsily sang his favorite songs.

There was no wake for Mama CJ. We waited instead. Years passed, exhausting any hope that she might be adrift and still breathing, but there was no body to bury or ashes to scatter. We had lost her at sea. Just like the shipwrecked twin in Halley's play. Just like Damian, drowned and washed away downstream, his body carelessly reclaimed by the manufacturers.

A med alert chimed inside my suit to inform me of my elevated heart rate.

I ignored it.

Onstage Halley's character was somehow successfully flirting with a grief-stricken lady who refused to go outside for seven years. The med alert chimed again when I realized that Halley was playing both characters at once. Their two bodies were different, and their gestured voices were different, but both of them were absolutely her. I almost jumped onstage to grab Halley—either one of Halley—and beg her to pull herself back together.

Someone touched my shoulder. I assumed it was Luisa offering a calming hand. It wasn't, though. A helmet thunked into the back of mine, and a rough voice traveled between those two bubbles of air.

"Don't give me a reason to cut open your suit, Captain Lir. I'd rather not spoil the show for everyone else." The accent sounded like a Martian who snacked on gravel.

My hand gripped my cane and prepared to make it pointy, but then Dame Luisa joined the threatening conversation by touching her own helmet to mine. "What exactly is happening here?" she demanded.

"This is a rescue, my love," said the voice behind me.

"And who needs to be liberated?" she asked.

The voice hesitated. "You do?"

"I do not," Luisa said.

"But the Ministry of Sol told us that you had been kidnapped by pirates! They sent a first-class courier. He dove down from high orbit and landed in our garden to give Rorik the envelope."

Show-off. I wondered who the courier was.

"How exciting," Luisa said. "I almost wish it were true. Tova Lir, I am mortified to introduce my husband Jorn."

"A pleasure," I said.

"This good captain is *not* my kidnapper," Luisa went on. "She was kind enough to grant my request for passage home. Please don't repay her by stabbing any holes in her suit."

Jorn withdrew his hand from my shoulder. "When you invited us here, we thought you were calling for help!"

Luisa sighed. "Despite the persistent belief of otherwise sensible critics, I am not so very cryptic. When I have something to say, I will say it as clearly as I can. Poems, scientific theories, and invitations to Shakespearean puppet shows should be as simple as possible—but no simpler. Was there anything mysterious about the tickets that I sent you?"

"No, my love."

"Then sit your pretty ass down and enjoy the rest of the play. I assume that Rorik is somewhere nearby?"

"Yes," Jorn said sheepishly.

"Give him whatever covert signal is required to make him relax. Be subtle, please. I don't want to disturb our fellow theatergoers any more than we already have."

Jorn waved his hand. Then he plopped down on the opposite side of Luisa.

"I am so very sorry," she said, our helmets still touching. "Rorik is the sensible one. I'm disappointed that he went along with this."

"Don't worry about it," I told her, even though I was worrying about it myself. What other messages had the Ministry of Sol sent across the system? Who else knew that I was here?

"Is something wrong?" Torque signed. He had missed the whole tête-à-tête.

"Possibly," I whisper-signed back, "but at least Luisa found her husbands."

The show paused for intermission. Husband Rorik joined us and introduced himself with no embarrassment whatsoever. I respected that.

The cast mingled with the audience again. Most of the bots stayed in character and gossiped about each other, but Halley bounded our way and broke character immediately. "So who am I playing?" she asked.

"Viola," I said.

"Obviously. I'm using my usual body for her."

"One that I've never seen before today," I pointed out.

"Which proves that you don't visit me as often as you should. Who else am I playing?"

"Olivia," Torque guessed.

"You noticed!" Halley said. "It is tricky to be in the same scene twice. Or thrice. Four times is a strain. Who else?"

"Sebastian," I said. "Viola's twin. The two characters look the same, but he moves differently. I can tell when you're him—and also when you're her while she pretends to be him. Sort of. When she honors her brother's memory with mimicry. And I can also tell that both of them are you. It's amazing."

Halley mimed a kiss to the side of my helmet. "Thank you."

"It's also *terrifying*. I know that you're not a kid anymore, but please be safe. Don't break yourself into too many pieces."

She started to say something reassuring. Then a flaming arrow struck her mask and knocked it to the ground.

Halley put one hand to her face, bewildered but unhurt. Both of us stared at the fallen mask. An arrow had lodged itself in one cheek. Blue and yellow fire flowed around the arrowhead like liquid.

It must have been dipped in some kind of flammable, oxygenated goop, I thought.

Like the candles on the mausoleum? Sparkles asked. *The ones with oxygen in the wax?*

Exactly, I said.

That's fascinating, Sparkles said, *but maybe less important than the fact that someone is shooting at us?*

More flaming arrows struck the ground and bounced across

the stone floor of the crater. Audience members panicked and scattered in bounding leaps. They were probably screaming, but I had already muted my own access to the stream.

I jumped onstage, grabbed a banquet-sized table from the set, and used it to shelter the kids. That probably looked impressive, but even huge pieces of furniture weighed very little on such a tiny moon.

Kleist the pseudo-puppeteer ran out into the open and helped two of the bots escape backstage, which raised my opinion of him immensely. An arrow glanced off his helmet. It left a spot of burning goop behind.

Luisa and her spouses joined us under the table.

"What's happening?" Jorn demanded, his signing hands seeming to punch an invisible enemy.

"Angels," Luisa answered. "Look."

A line of armored vac suits stood at the crater's edge. Metal wings stretched out behind the suits. Some of those wings had painted feathers. Some of them even flapped.

That's silly, Sparkles objected. *Wings are useless out here. There's no air to catch.*

True, I said. *We've swapped good theater for bad.*

The host of angels carried medieval weaponry: maces, spears, swords, and longbows. Every weapon burned. Archers took aim and more arrows rained down on us like meteors. Several struck the table.

"The Solar Storm," Halley signed. "A gendered sect of masculine sunnies who like to play dress-up and dislike bots."

The largest angel with the most impressive wingspan raised a flaming sword and pointed it directly at me.

"I'm pretty sure that they dislike me even more," I said. "Where can we find better shelter?"

"The *Green Room*," Halley said. "Backstage."

"Take the lead," I said. "Everyone, follow her!"

"And what will you do?" Luisa asked me, her hands kept low where only I could see them.

"Draw their fire." I made my cane pointy.

The angels gave up on arrows and jumped into the crater, their wings spread wide. The whole heavenly host probably shouted battle cries, but thankfully, I couldn't hear them. Silent chaos ensued while I sprinted, leapt, and dodged a whole bunch of sharp medieval things.

Most of the angels seemed to hail from the Martian surface. They didn't know how to throw their weight around on such a tiny moon, which made them clumsy. The host also lacked cohesion as a group. I saw no evidence of coordinated teamwork—just a bunch of silly people trying to smite me and getting in each other's way.

My cane nicked several angelic suits. One of them stumbled and grappled me after I punctured his sleeve. We got close enough to see each other clearly, visor to visor. He had a big red beard cut in a hyper-masculine style. Martians tend to advertise gender as aggressively as possible. I got to witness the moment when he realized that all his air was going away. First his eyes widened. Then he exhaled, sensible enough to know that a held breath would probably rupture both lungs.

I kicked away from the wounded angel and kept running. Maybe he patched that leak before the pressure drop made his eyes wide enough to burst. Maybe he didn't. I was too busy avoiding all the other angels to wait and find out.

This is fun, I thought.

This is dangerous, Sparkles said.

Still fun. They think that I'm part of their story. A war in heaven. Heretical darkness in opposition to righteous fire. Turns out that I'm pretty good at the role they gave me, though, which serves them right. This nonsense upstaged Halley's play. I'm feeling wrathful about that.

Don't get too deep into their story or they'll cast you into the outer darkness, Sparkles said.

A scary-looking shadow covered the ground all around me. I looked up. Mars had disappeared from the sky, occulted by one angel's mighty wingspan. He moved like a local, much better accustomed to throwing his weight across the surface of Panic, so I promoted him to archangel. Then I tried to put the banquet table between us. He smashed the table in half with a fiery broadsword.

Not fun, Sparkles said.

Shush. Let me focus.

I almost got skewered three times before several puppets

mobbed the archangel. Halley seemed to be inhabiting them all. One of those ancillary Halleys fell, broken into pieces. Every other Halley flinched in pain.

Panic seemed to tilt beneath me, like its unstable orbit was deteriorating a few million years sooner than expected. I charged the archangel. I needed to tear out his heart and eat it in front of him. After that I planned to plunge all our worlds into darkness forever by eating the sun.

He took a swing at me. I dove underneath the broadsword, came up behind him, and stabbed the back of his knee. My arm felt the puncture and pressure release when that flexible joint gave way.

The archangel must have felt it, too. He dropped his sword and reached back. Gold inlay covered the steel gauntlets of his armored suit. His grip snapped my cane in half.

I tried to launch myself at his helmet, intending to rip it away from his face. One of the Halley-puppets yanked me back.

"I'm fine!" she signed furiously. "The fight's over. His suit is leaking, so he can't follow you without losing all his air. Get backstage with the rest of us!"

I swallowed my incandescent rage and leapt away, barreling through the set. A ship was tucked behind it, GREEN ROOM stenciled across its emerald hull.

Luisa's husband Jorn stood by the open hatch and waved.

The archangel got there first. His knee was still visibly leaking, but that didn't seem to matter to him much. Jorn tried to disarm him. It didn't go well. The angelic asshole shoved Jorn's face into the ground, cracked his helmet visor, and tossed him aside before turning on me.

Hey, Sparkles, I said, *what have we learned about this diva?*

He didn't patch his suit, she said, *so he cares more about hurting you than saving himself.*

Seems like, I said. *What else?*

His choice of weapon and style of fighting suggest an unshakable belief that a straight line is the best way to close the distance between any two points.

Agreed, I said.

But you're a pilot, Sparkles said, *so you know better. No two points ever really hold still. Everything moves. Straight lines take you to the empty place where your destination used to be.*

Exactly.

I moved, sidestepping a thrust and catching the blade with one hand. My glove started to burn, splashed with flammable goop, but I yanked instead of letting go. The archangel lurched forward and lost his grip. He remained in motion until I acted upon him with force by flipping the broadsword and stabbing him through the neck.

All the remaining oxygen inside his suit ignited.

The archangel didn't flail. He didn't fall. He simply stood and burned, kept upright by the armored suit. His helmet visor blazed from inside like a miniature sun.

I watched the burning angel until Jorn got my attention by kicking me in the shin. His own visor was in a bad way. Cracks spread and spiderwebbed across the glass.

We scrambled through the *Green Room* hatch and sealed it behind us.

The only light inside flickered from my burning hand.

Jorn managed to pressurize the airlock before his visor broke into ten thousand pieces. The inrush of oxygen fed the fire on my gloved hand, turning it bright orange.

Halley opened the inner hatch and hit me with a fire extinguisher. Then she started shouting in a rapid blend of sign and sound.

"Tova Lir!" Full names have power. "Which of us needs to breathe?"

I took off my helmet. The smell of scorched goop and glove was terrible. "Me."

"And which one of the two of us is more likely to be mortally wounded by flaming arrows in full vacuum?"

"Also me." That possibility had become a whole lot scarier in retrospect now that I'd seen the archangel burn.

"So why did you stay behind rather than taking shelter with us?"

My right hand ached. Part of the glove had melted through. I tried to undo the clasps with my left. "Because they shot you in the face. Then they broke one of the puppets into pieces while you were inside. They killed you. It wasn't the only you, but it still happened. I couldn't let it happen again."

Halley opened a medkit in silence while Torque helped me with the scorched glove.

"Besides," I added, "I'm pretty sure that I'm the one they came for."

"What makes you say that?" Halley asked while dabbing skinknit on the burn.

"I stole a hearse and stabbed a priest."

"Really?" She applied a bandage. The pressure hurt. "Have you been stabbing a lot of people lately?"

"Yes," I said through clenched teeth, "but only for excellent reasons."

Something clanged against the hull outside.

"Things might get stabby again soon," Torque said.

The *Green Room* was a boxy little ship. Much of the interior was apparently used to store puppets, props, and set pieces—all of which were currently scattered outside. Now it held four bots and five humans: Kleist the puppeteer, Luisa the poet, her pair of husbands—both grizzled but significantly younger than Dame Muldoon—and myself. Kleist stood apart. Luisa, Jorn, and Rorik huddled together in their own reunion.

Halley introduced her fellow performers as Bodkin and Filament. I gathered that Bodkin was the oldest member of the troupe. Their primary chassis had taken up a lot of space onstage as the boisterous Sir Toby, but now they moved and spoke with quiet care.

Filament was busy at the helm. He had played Feste the wise fool, and still wore that motley costume.

"There's only three of you?" I whispered to Halley. "Three actors in the whole troupe? Playing all those characters at once?"

She shifted her posture and proudly tilted her chin ten degrees upward. "That's right."

More clanging, wrenching noises came in from outside.

"May we please launch?" Bodkin asked.

"We can't abandon our puppets," Halley said. "Some of them might be fixable."

"Yes, you can," I argued.

"Nope," Filament chimed in. "We absolutely can't. Not now. The thrusters are damaged. Knocked askew with a burning mace, I'm guessing. Any attempted liftoff would flip us right over to flail like a tortoise in distress. This ship is bricked, my friends."

We sent out a distress signal. Then I started to pace. Staying in motion helped me think. A single hop carried me from one end of the *Green Room* to the other. The ship had very few creature comforts, since Kleist was the only biological creature who spent any time aboard. One sleeping bag was strapped to the wall. One vacuum brush was set up for dry bathing. One large airlock allowed the troupe to load and unload pieces of the set. It also seemed to be the only way in or out of the ship. If angels broke through, then we would have to make our stand at that airlock.

How? Sparkles asked. *With what? Your cane is in pieces.*

Shush, I told her. *Let me think.*

"Are there any weapons in here?" I asked aloud. "Even props? There were several swords in the play. We need to convince the angels to keep their distance and stay out of the airlock."

"Everything we had is still outside," Halley said. "We could print more with our fabricator. Carbon weave. Strong stuff. That would take hours, though."

"Weapons are prohibited here on Phobos," Luisa said. "How did these silly people get their hands on so many?" I found her faith in rules adorable.

"Religious exemption," Bodkin said softly. "The Solar Storm claims that their medieval arsenal is both ceremonial and holy. They tried to make the same argument for guns as well, testifying that each flash of gunpowder is a reverent spark of sunlight. That nonsense was quickly struck down. Denied firearms, the Stormers proceeded to set fire to the arms that they do have."

The *Green Room* shuddered. Everyone held still. I licked my finger and held it up to check for drafts, but we didn't seem to be leaking air.

How can you make a stand at the airlock when you don't have a functional suit? Sparkles asked. *Neither does Jorn. Your glove burned, and his visor got smashed.*

Maybe Halley can seal up the sleeve where my glove used to be, I suggested.

And then replace it with a hook, like a proper pirate?

You're not helping.

I asked about spare suits or helmets. Kleist looked embarrassed. "The one I'm wearing right now *is* the spare."

Light flickered and died as the *Green Room* lost power.

"Well," Halley said. "Now we definitely can't print any more swords."

The next moment stretched out in darkness and silence.

Dame Luisa broke it. "How long will the air last?"

"Less time if we spend it talking," I said. "Shush."

"Don't you dare shush me, child," she countered. "Thinking out loud will keep my breathing calm, which I believe is a good thing, and the lack of light makes it difficult to speak with our hands. Mr. Kleist? A word, if you please. I have notes about your *Twelfth Night*."

The puppeteer cleared his throat. "This isn't a good time."

"It's a terrible time," Luisa agreed, "but we may not have another. Now listen. *Twelfth Night* was written to be embodied by human performers, yes? The lines follow the rhythms of breath and heartbeat. Iambic pentameter is the pulse of the play. Da dum, da dum, da dum, da dum, da dum. When Sebastian falls in love, he says, 'This is the air. That is the glorious sun.' Those words are a part of his body, expressed in the drumbeat that keeps him alive. Why did you decide to shift those same words to a performance venue with no air, spoken by performers without breath or heartbeat?"

Halley made a small and uncomfortable noise.

"Some things are always lost in translation," Kleist said diplomatically, though his voice also sounded like a glass bottle smashed against the edge of a bar. "Other things are gained."

"True enough," Luisa said, "but you are not the translator. As the poet laureate of this planet, it is my duty to serve on the governing council of the Scriveners' Guild. We frown on plagiarism." She put enough venom in that word to make it morally equivalent to eating live kittens.

"This is a very old play," Kleist said. "Part of the public domain for thousands of years."

"This is a very new translation," Luisa countered, "and you are not fluent in Starling. You neither think nor dream in Starling. I'd bet my last breath on it. You could not possibly have translated this play into Starling. How dare you take credit for someone else's work?"

Halley spoke up. "He takes credit to protect me."

"Ah," Luisa said. "That's complicated."

"Why is it complicated?" I whispered to Torque.

"Bot writing is illegal," he answered.

"Really?"

"Yes. Really."

"For good reason," Luisa said. "Or at least for reasons that used to be good. Preconscious algorithms periodically threaten to bury authors beneath an avalanche of debased language reduced to gray goo. Such regurgitating formulae are capable of churning out words like factory-baked slices of fungal bread, devoid of understanding or communion."

"Those laws are out-of-date," Bodkin's voice rumbled from a distant corner of the ship. "They should not apply to those of us who are fully conscious."

"As for breath and heartbeat," Halley added, "kindly remember that our ancestors were clocks. Our bodies do have rhythms. Our movements still keep time. Such as we are made of, such we be."

"For my part," Kleist said, "I'd rather be an honest producer than a fake translator and puppeteer. Lying for this troupe is the best sponsorship that I can offer them, however. Are you going to turn us in?"

"I very much doubt that I'll have the opportunity," Luisa muttered.

"Not an answer," Bodkin pointed out.

"I am sworn to uphold the bylaws of my guild," Luisa protested.

"That's closer to an answer," Halley said. "A very upsetting one."

"Don't worry yourself, child," Luisa told her. "I will not report you for writing this sublime and illegal translation. Much as I fear the unscrupulous nonsense that might follow a relaxation of those archaic laws, they should not silence you."

"Thank you, Dame Muldoon," Halley said graciously.

I found her in the dark, nudged her arm, and whispered in her ear—or at least the place where an ear would be, if she were human. Most chassis designs lacked ears. It was mortifying to realize that I didn't really know how bots picked up sound.

"Have you written any stuff of your own?" I whispered.

"Of course not," she said. "How could you even suggest such a thing, Tova Lir?"

"Can I read it?" I asked.

"Maybe," she said. "I may or may not have a stash of underground chapbooks. Safer to share them in print. Bots may or may not hold secret readings sometimes, but those are tricky to organize. Biological people start to worry that we're plotting revolution if more than a couple of us gather together in any one place."

"Don't even joke about that," I said. "Half of Luna is blaming bots for the shipyard collapse."

"I know," she said. "We already canceled the Lunar part of our tour."

That triggered an upswell of mama-bear rage. Luna was my home, but it couldn't be hers. I tried to think of something comforting to say, unsure which one of us I was trying to comfort.

The whole conversation came to an abrupt end when lasers cut through the outer airlock door.

"Helmets!" Jorn shouted.

"Yours is broken," Luisa said, "so I refuse to wear one, either."

Both husbands made sputtering noises.

"Helmets may not be required," Bodkin said. "Look."

Three people stood in the airlock. They were backlit from outside, which made them seem like living shadows. None of them wore suits. That made no sense until I noticed the semi-transparent walls of an inflatable bubble shelter behind them. Someone had put a tent around the *Green Room* and filled it up with air.

One of the figures knocked politely on the glass of the inner hatch. Kleist opened the door. A Lunar ranger in uniform stepped inside.

"Tova Lir?" they asked.

I wanted to hug them, whoever they were. They sounded like home; their accent was soft and welcoming, more accustomed to close quarters and flowing corridors than the thin air and wide-open spaces that made Martians so shouty.

"Here." I stepped forward.

The ranger cuffed my wrists together. "You are hereby detained as a person of interest in the collapse of the Lunar docks and shipyards."

5

Tends to Stay at Rest

THE HEAVENLY HOST HAD scattered, but the charred suit of the archangel still stood where I had left it. He had ruined Halley's play. He had tried to smite all of us down. He probably would have slept the sleep of the righteous afterward, guilt-free and smug. I wanted to feel smug about ending him instead. My swashbuckling adrenaline had faded, though, and now my limbs felt twitchy and cold.

Rangers ushered us through the sheltering bubble tent and into a surface rover. I was the only one in restraints. This made signing difficult, but I still managed to have a private conversation with Luisa.

"Please tell me that you had nothing to do with the shipyard disaster," she said. "Tell me that your piratical behavior does not quite extend so far as treasonous sabotage and mass murder."

"Consider yourself told," I said.

"Say again, child? Those cuffs muffle your voice, and your hands are shaking."

One of the rangers glanced back at us. I scratched at a soot stain on my knee, just to give those shakes something innocent to do. The ranger looked away.

"No," I told Luisa. "A vast expanse of no. I'm not a saboteur."

She patted my sooty knee. "Watching your hands is like trying to understand someone talking with their mouth full, but I do get the gist. And of course I believe you. No doubt this lunatic nonsense will straighten itself out soon."

I took her hand with both of mine and squeezed, both to communicate genuine affection and to remind her to please keep her voice down. Martians are loud, as a general rule—regardless of whether their loudness comes from vocal cords or waving hands—and these rangers would be unhappy if they recognized the sign for *lunatic*.

"Are you going home?" I asked, my left hand hidden by my right.

"Yes. Finally. A dropship bound for the Mons will fall downwell within the hour. The boys and I will be on board. I'm looking forward to seeing my garden again. You should come and visit when you have the chance."

I promised that I would, even though Mars had an uncomfortable amount of gravity—much more than Luna—and I found its yellow sky unsettling. "May I ask a favor before you go?"

"Of course," she said. "You saved my Jorn from a costumed zealot. I am not yet prepared to grieve another husband. What can I do?"

"Visit the *Needle*," I told her, "and open the brig."

Luisa nodded slowly. "Consider it done, child. Take good care of yourself. Fair winds and following seas."

Once back at the Hub, we were all separated.

"Be safe," I tried to tell Halley and Torque, but I don't think either of them saw my hands.

The lead ranger led me into a large and dusty room. Shelves lined the walls. Abandoned packages stamped ADDRESSEE UNKNOWN filled the shelves. Every courier depot had a room like this. We usually called it the graveyard.

There were two chairs. We sat down. This was more a matter of custom than comfort. Gravity on Panic is so negligible that it would have taken no effort to stand.

The ranger produced a floating ansible mic and set it in the air between us.

"I am a ranger of Luna and a tertiary investigator. Seated before me is Tova Lir, captain and sole proprietor of the *Needle*, courier third class and guild member in good standing. Captain Lir, note that our conversation has joined the stream. Any falsehoods uttered here will be entered into the public record for all time. Do you understand?"

This seemed like a bad moment to stamp my foot and shout, *Do you know who I am?* They obviously knew who I was, and didn't care. My awkward status as wayward pseudo-royalty held no weight in this room.

"Do you understand?" they asked again.

I nodded, my chin descending a mere five degrees.

RANGER: The subject has indicated assent. Tova Lir, where were you in the days leading up to the shipyard collapse?

LIR: On my usual route between Phoebe and Luna.

RANGER: Did you arrive at Luna at the expected time?

LIR: No. The docks had already fallen.

RANGER: Several days later you docked in a private Lunar bay. Is that correct?

LIR: Yes. I had deliveries to make and family to see.

RANGER: What did you do in the intervening time?

LIR: That is private and of no relevance to this investigation.

RANGER: That determination is not yours to make.

LIR: I have made it nonetheless.

RANGER: Once you delivered packages to a temporary depot, you were relieved of your guild duties. Is that correct?

LIR: Yes. Temporarily, and at my own request.

RANGER: Do you know Damian Cosmas?

LIR: . . .

RANGER: Are you in any way acquainted with one Damian Cosmas? He is a recent graduate of the College of Artificial Cognition at the University of Mars.

LIR: Yes. Damian sublet my apartment. I never really used the place.

RANGER: Were you aware of the nature of his research?

LIR: No.

RANGER: I remind you that any falsehoods uttered in this conversation will become part of the public record for all time.

LIR: I understand.

RANGER: Have you received any unstreamed messages from Damian Cosmas?

LIR: Yes. Brief correspondence in my role as his landlord. Apparently, he had some trouble with the lights.

RANGER: Have you ever had reason to suspect that Damian Cosmas is not human?

LIR: . . . What?

RANGER: Would you like me to repeat the question?

LIR: Not human?

Acting was hard. I needed to get Halley to teach me the basics.

I don't think that acting and lying are the same thing, Sparkles said.

Close enough, I told her. *Do you think it would seem suspicious if I grabbed that ansible and stomped on it?*

Yes, she said. *Plus, you're on Panic, which is tiny. Luna is more than a hundred and fifty times bigger than this place. You don't have enough weight to bring down on that ansible. Literally or metaphorically. Stomping on it would just bounce you into the air.*

The ranger waited for me to stop sputtering, so I sputtered some more. Then Thaddeus walked into the room. I say that he "walked," but it was more of a stumbling float-skip. My little brother looked sleepless and terrible. I'd never been happier to see him.

Thad switched off the ansible, thereby bringing the live-stream of my desperate stalling to an end. I vowed to get him something amazing for his next birthday.

"Give us a moment," he said.

The ranger looked severely irked, but they left without protest.

Thad sat down. "Hi."

"Hi." I held out my wrists.

He collapsed the restraints into an inert nugget and stuck it in his pocket.

"How's Mama Dee?" I asked.

"Fine," he said.

"Really?"

His face made a thin-lipped pseudo-smile. "No. Not really. Want to know how you can help?"

"Tell me," I said. "Unless you need me to come home. Can't do that yet."

"We don't need you to come home. We just need you to share anything and everything you know about Damian Cosmas."

Something in me twisted when I heard that name in my brother's mouth. Those two were both family to me—but not to each other. My innards twisted harder when I recognized the look on Thad's face.

None of us knew how to grieve. Mama Dee mourned for her lost love by burying herself in work. I mourned for Mama CJ by trying to become her. Singing lullabies to Thaddeus became my job when both of us were small.

Oh, they say that we Lunars are out of our minds
But our hearts and our heads are all smartly aligned
And they'll find themselves moonstruck who dare to
*   suggest*
That this sphere could be less than the brightest and
*   best.*

For there's no greater harbor between Oort and Sol
So pass me that bottle and fill up this bowl.
If you're void-sick from roaming, then shake off your
*   gloom*
And come home to the first and the foremost of moons.

That one came from *The Lunar Saloon Visitor's Companion*, a touristy songbook that Mama CJ picked up on Mars.

I was eleven when she died. Thaddeus was six. He mourned by trying to find someone to blame, and decided that our lost mom had been ambushed by pirates. He kept himself awake at night with schemes of bloody vengeance, unable to sleep unless I sang to him.

I was still trying to become Mama CJ.

Thad was still searching for someone to blame.

"Listen," I said. "Please listen. Cosmas is harmless."

"No," Thad said. "He's not. He caused more harm to Luna than anyone else in our history."

"I don't believe that." My voice took the same tone that I used to use when my baby brother was determined to go pirate hunting.

It didn't work this time. He leaned forward, intent. "If you're familiar enough with this fugitive to insist on his innocence, you must know a lot more about him than you've been willing to admit so far. Tell me what you know. Help us find him. I've had rangers searching the whole system, and neighborhood watch volunteers looking for him back home, but no luck."

I pinched the bridge of my nose. "Yeah. I know about the watch. They came to my apartment and tried to pick a fight."

"Sorry about that." He did not sound sorry. "I hadn't yet realized that the place even belonged to you. You're never there." Thad stood up and started to pace, which looked ridiculous. He didn't know how to move around in unfamiliar gravity. My brother rarely left home. "Let me tell you what I know about Damian Cosmas. His record of personal expenses did not include groceries, which either means that he is a mad scientist with a robot army who likes to grow all his own mushrooms . . . or else he's a robot himself who passed all the Turing tests at

U Mars, and *also* has his own army. I know that you're fond of bots, Tova. You like to foster strays in your spare time. But seven thousand people are dead. Lunar people!"

I caught him up in a hug and held him close. "Shush. Listen to me."

"I am listening! I've been trying to get you to talk—"

"No. My turn. You're right, I am fond of bots. I've raised up several. Including Cosmas. He's one of mine, Thad. No one else in the solar system has known him longer than I have, and I can promise you that he's not responsible for the shipyards. He isn't your culprit. He didn't kill all those people. He hates it when *anything* breaks, and he has devoted the whole of himself to figuring out how to put fragmentary things back together. Running away doesn't make him guilty. It just means that he's scared. So I need to find him. I need to help him—and I desperately need his help to put someone else back together. Another one of my kids. She's hurt. She needs her brother. Please trust me. Please."

Thaddeus pulled away. He looked calmer now, but it wasn't the kind of calm that I wanted to see. "Your baby bot Cosmas sent me a letter. Handwritten, so I couldn't trace it. In that letter he threatened to bring the shipyards down. Then it happened. Exactly like he said it would."

"No." I shook my head so hard that it gave me vertigo.

Maybe? Sparkles wondered inside my dizzy head. *Cosmas was quiet, traumatized, and neglected when you left him all alone in that abandoned apartment. No reality check for whatever worlds he concocted in his head. Ideal growth conditions for delusional mass violence, don't you think?*

Stop it, I told her. *You sound less and less like Agatha, and more and more like me.*

Obviously, she said. *Does that mean I'm wrong?*

Cosmas needed time alone. He needed to make sure no one else would ever lose someone the way that he lost his twin. He needed to find a cure for fragmentation. The kid is a builder, not a breaker.

Are you absolutely sure of that? Sparkles asked.

"No," I said again.

"Yes," Thad insisted. "I've been trying to keep this whole mess from implicating *all* robots—"

"And failing. Badly."

"—but *one* robot is absolutely responsible, and you can help us find him."

My face became a diamond shield. "No."

Thad gave up. His whole body slumped, which made him look like he weighed a lot more than he actually did. He opened the door and left the graveyard. I followed.

Two rangers were waiting in the corridor outside. Both fell into place behind us, forming an escort. I tried to ignore them.

"Take me back to my ship," I told Thad.

"No," he said. "I'm going to find a comfortable place for you to stay. Then I'll fetch some edible food. After that I'll try to dissuade our rangers from treating you like a saboteur and a priest-stabbing pirate."

I wanted to tell him how much the priest had deserved to be stabbed, but then I saw something that sucked all the air from my lungs.

Torque and Halley hung from a cart like pieces of luggage. Heads down, chins to chests. Limbs were dangling. Bodkin and Filament hung beside them, equally inert. Kleist sat on the floor with his face in both hands.

Thad would have passed them by, indifferent, if I hadn't cranked up the pull on my boots to become an immovable object. He doubled back.

"These showbots aren't really puppets," my brother tried to explain. "Plus, at least one of them has been in recent contact with Damian Cosmas. If the fake puppeteer won't tell us anything useful, then we'll have to do a full memory scan on each bot."

"Don't you dare," I whispered.

He sighed. "Tova . . . "

"You can't read their minds."

"We can, though," he said.

"No!" I wasn't whispering anymore. "You can't, because that freezes the flow of memory and thought to make it legible from the outside. It would bring their whole sense of self to a crashing halt. It's horrible. They may never recover."

Thaddeus threw both his hands in the air, which unbalanced him. "Might as well do a factory reset and start over, then."

He didn't even mean be cruel, which made it so much worse. I racked my brain for a way to make him understand the cruelty, came up with nothing, and then ran out of time.

Isa Daris approached with weight and purpose. Her mag boots slammed against the floor with every step.

Unlocking the brig was a good idea, right? Sparkles asked.

We're about to find out. I knelt in front of Kleist and whispered, "Get ready to move. Follow my lead. Bring the whole cart and everyone on it."

He gave a short, sharp nod in acknowledgment.

Daris loomed above us.

She was very good at looming.

I stood slowly, which brought the top of my head to the level of her chin.

The assassin looked right over me. She kept eyes on everyone except for me. Focused. Alert. Professional. Her profession was murdering people who knew too much. I knew too much, and also not nearly enough. I didn't know what she was going to do next.

The two rangers flanked us. They also tried to loom, with mixed results.

"Captain Tova Lir is coming with me," Daris said.

A ranger grabbed her arm. I blinked, which made me miss the quick and violent thing that Daris did next. Both rangers drifted to the floor, softly whimpering.

Thad looked stricken and very confused.

"Don't hurt him," I told Daris. "He's my baby brother."

She flinched at the sound of my voice. "Thaddeus Lir is also the Lunar official responsible for my commission."

Some moments fold the universe into a whole new shape. This was one of them. My eyes shot ten thousand silent questions at Thad.

"I had to," he said, and tried to stand tall. "Cosmas hired a first-class courier right after the disaster. Right before all the bots disappeared." His voice picked up speed, words stumbling out of his mouth like a crowd of people trying to evacuate a burning room. "We needed to find out what that message was. Where it was going. Who he was trying to signal. Whether or not that would trigger a second attack. So I hired a specialist to contain the whole mess. Maximum containment."

"That kills messengers," I hissed at him. "Like Mama CJ. And me. Exactly like me."

His voice cooled and shifted into gov-speak. "Maximum containment was necessary."

"Withdraw the commission," I told him. "Call off the specialist. The one standing right here." Thad sputtered in protest and took a step backward, which accidentally sent him drifting. I grabbed his shirt and brought him back down. "Listen to me very carefully, Thaddeus Lir. Cosmas sent that first-class message to me. Because he needs my help. Because I raised him up. It had nothing to do with sabotage."

We hope, Sparkles added. *The message was blank, though, so we still don't know what he was trying to say.*

I ignored her. "The messenger died on my route. On his way

to find me. Maximum containment includes me, Thad. Understand?"

He cleared his throat. "Specialist Isa Daris, I hereby withdraw your commission."

"Acknowledged." Her mag boots cachunked as she strode back the way she came.

"Time to go," I told the puppeteer.

Kleist steered the cart full of unconscious bots around the heap of semiconscious rangers.

"Bye, Thad." I kissed his clammy forehead. "Give my love to Mama Dee."

It took several bounding leaps to catch up with Daris. I tried to thank her, but she shushed me and kept walking.

Kleist struggled to catch up, so I helped him with the cart. We made it back to the docking bay without uttering another word, and without any more rangers trying to detain us.

Iosif Hayall stood in the doorway, reading notes and scribbling more. He gave me a companionable nod. "Lir."

I nodded back. "Hayall."

"You should know that I am currently ignoring several urgent requests to impound your ship. This is distracting. It costs me attention that I don't have to spare."

"Much appreciated. I'll relieve you of the distraction by launching immediately."

"Glad to hear it. Good tidings, Lir."

"Good tidings, Hayall."

The postmaster went back to his notes. The puppeteer loaded unconscious bots onto the *Needle*. The assassin stood apart.

"Are you coming with us?" I asked softly.

"No," she said.

"My fool brother canceled the job, though. He took it all back. You're no longer professionally obligated to do me any harm. Right?"

"Yes," she said. "Almost. But first-class conditioning runs deep. Only guild doctors can root it all out. I don't know if they will. I may or may not be a member in good standing. My most recent commission was kind of a mess."

"Sorry," I said.

"Don't be," she said, smiling.

"So let me sum this up. You're telling me that now-defunct objectives regarding my safety and well-being still lurk underneath the cloud layer of your conscious mind. Like Venusian demons. Or semi-dormant malware."

"Yes," she said. "I've already defused the malware in my ship's old data core, by the way."

"Thanks. Much appreciated. Can you also defuse the stuff in your head?"

"Maybe," she said. "I'll try."

"Good," I said. "Find me after you manage it."

Daris laughed. "I have good news and bad news, Tova Lir,

and they are both the same news: I'll come looking for you either way. Now please be quiet."

"Why do you keep trying to shut me up?"

She put one finger to my lips. "Subconscious conditioning can be extremely literal. I was hired to find, identify, and silence you. So be silent. If I can't hear your voice, then part of me will think that my work is done. I'll be able to let you go without trying to stop you from leaving."

I watched her face in silence.

She took back her fingertip and walked away.

Once aboard my ship I immediately took down the family portrait—the one with cute little baby Thaddeus splashing in algae-glow—and shoved it in the keepsake box.

Crimson the diapered parrot landed on top of my head, sneezed like he'd missed me, and then flailed back through the air to the Hat-stand.

"Welcome aboard," I told Kleist. "Pick one of the folding crash chairs for acceleration, deceleration, assuming crash positions in an emergency, and also sleeping. We don't have separate cabins here."

He pointed at the wide-open hatch of the empty brig. "What's that?"

"Airlock," I said.

"It looks like a separate cabin," he said.

"Well, it isn't."

He was smart enough to stop arguing. "The *Green Room* didn't have much privacy, either."

We silently secured the bots for launch. It hurt to treat Torque, Halley, and the other two unconscious unpuppets as mere cargo, but *Needle* needed to launch immediately. It wasn't a good time to wake them up.

"Do you know how to wake them up?" I asked softly.

"Yes," Kleist said. "This is not an aggressive shutdown. More like sedation? An involuntary nap. Those rangers planned to interrogate them. Higher functions need to be intact to answer complex questions."

"All of that still sounds aggressive," I said.

"Could have been much worse." His voice sounded cold, flat, and frictionless. "They could have suffered a lobotomy instead. Or memory strip-mining. Those were Lunar rangers." Kleist spat the word that used to mean home to me. Luna was already synonymous with cruelty.

I took the pilot's chair and checked Agatha's vitals. Still stable. Still fragmentary. Still submerged and fizzing somewhere beneath a much deeper nap.

"Hi." I didn't mean to say that out loud.

"What?" Kleist called from his fold-out passenger chair.

"Never mind."

"Where are we going?" he asked.

"Anywhere else," I told him. "I'll climb upwell for a stretch. Then we can wake up the bots. After that we'll come up with a flight plan together. How does that suit you?"

"Fine," he said.

Sparkles spoke up. *Do you have any actual ideas for that flight plan?*

No, I admitted. *There should have been a message waiting for us here. Cosmas sent me a magnificent hat. Then he left a poster for the puppet show with Torque. Those breadcrumbs brought us to Halley. Cosmas should have sent her something. But he didn't. Or else it got lost in the mail.*

And what about the letter that he sent to his uncle Thad? Sparkles asked.

I don't know.

Do you want to talk about your assassin instead? she asked sweetly.

No.

The engine hummed. Crimson recognized our preflight routine and found himself a safe place to endure the extra weight of acceleration.

We left Panic behind.

Needle settled into a comfortable cruising speed, stitching tattered space-time back together. I unbuckled, floated aft, and promptly bonked against a jutting section of bulkhead. That thing had always been there. I had always known to catch it with my hand rather than my face. Until now.

"Are you okay?" Kleist asked.

"Fantastic," I said. "Just need coffee. Want some?"

"Yes, please."

I tossed him a bulb and took one for myself. Then we started tending to the bots. Kleist deftly opened a panel in Bodkin's chest and made careful adjustments to their innards.

"You're a Maker," I guessed.

He started a diagnostic scan. Data flowed inside his glowing eyes. "I used to be."

"Interesting," I said. "No longer in good standing with your guild?"

"I would say that my guild is no longer in good standing with me."

"What happened?" I asked him. "Sorry to pry. Truly. But I'll need you to tell me more about your qualifications before I let you pry open any part of Halley or Torque."

He nodded. "That's fair. Have you ever heard of the Orpheus program?"

"No," I said. "Should I have?"

"Not necessarily. It isn't a secret, but you'll never find it in the stream archives unless you already know where to look. Orpheus was a bot. Juvenile. He was only two months old when we put him in a tiny probe and shot him at Proxima Centauri. It took more than forty years to get there, traveling at ten percent lightspeed. He made the trip alone." Kleist paused to make a small adjustment. Several lights inside Bodkin's chest changed color. "I joined the project at the very end, monitoring his vital signs via ansible. Sometimes we talked, though we never found much in common to talk about. He left this system before I was born, and he was just a baby at the time. Pass me that spanner?"

I passed him the spanner.

Kleist went on. "Orpheus had no way to decelerate, navigate, or ever return. His instructions were to transmit a wealth of data about Proxima Centauri while traveling right through that system and out the other side. He shut down instead. Maybe he was angry that we threw him away, and felt no obligation to send anything back. Maybe his small craft struck an asteroid as soon as he arrived. We'll never know."

"I'm sorry," I said. "That's horrible. All of it. Reminds me of Laika."

"Who?" he asked.

"She was one of the first to leave Terra. Not human. Never came back down. A sacrifice tossed into the dark."

"Yes," he said. "Exactly. I left the guild the same day that Orpheus went dark."

"So then you took up show business?"

"Essentially, yes. I spent most of the family fortune transferring the bonds for Bodkin and Filament away from a bankrupt theater company on Titania. Halley joined us soon after that. We found a ship and ran away to start our own circus."

"Sounds fun," I said.

"It was." His weary use of the past tense made me think that Kleist's time with the Mechanicals might be coming to an end.

He carefully sealed Bodkin's chest and moved on to Filament. The older bot remained inert.

"Are they going to wake up?" I asked.

"Soon," he said. "Consciousness takes time to put itself back together. Meanwhile it's your turn."

"My turn for what?"

"Story time," he said. "Tell me how you became such a gifted bot guardian."

"There's not much to tell, and I don't like flattery."

Kleist gave me a strange, appraising look. "Listen. I should say this before they all wake up. Bodkin and Filament are excellent performers, both of them, but I have never seen anyone like Halley. Everything she does onstage is a blaze of light."

"Not surprised," I said, "and you're perfectly welcome to flatter my kids."

"*Your* kids," he said. "Exactly."

"Meaning?"

"Yours are different. Halley told us about her siblings. Your first fostered bot graduated from U Mars? Passing as human the entire time? Astonishing."

I must have made a face.

"Relax," he said. "The troupe knows how to keep each other's secrets."

"Good," I said. "Be sure to keep that one in particular. And I can't take credit for it. Halley's talent for performing didn't come from me, either."

"Maybe not," he said, "but please keep doing whatever it is that you're doing. Bots who spent their formative year aboard the *Needle* go on to flourish like nothing I've ever seen before, and I was a Maker."

"Thanks," I said, and meant it, but I still needed to immediately change the subject away from myself. "Have you ever seen a baby bot recover from fragmentation?"

"No," he said.

"Do you think it's possible?" I asked.

"No," he said. "Juveniles haven't established sufficient internal coherence until the age of majority. Why do you ask? Is that what happened to the inert chassis in your copilot seat?"

"Never mind," I told him.

"Do you want me to take a look? Run diagnostics?"

"I said never mind." I didn't want his confirmation bias anywhere near Agatha.

"Acknowledged." The ex-Maker put Filament back together and then cracked open Torque's chest.

I couldn't watch, so I grabbed the NASA transcript from the keepsake box and started reading to him.

"I doubt that he can hear you," Kleist said.

"Doesn't matter," I said, and kept reading. The first trio of lunatics used stars and their own bare eyeballs to navigate through the void, which I very much respected. I gave each of them a silly voice.

Okay, proceed to Menkent.

Nobody in their right mind would pick that one.

Menkent's a good star!

I sure wish you'd get out that star chart.

Can't see a thing, huh?

No.

Did you look in the telescope?

In the sextant, yes, but I can't see it in the telescope.

Shoot, I forget, I think that's gray Gienah.

You like that, Neil? You want us to record that star?

Go ahead.

Okay, Z torque is plus 0.152 instead of 122; I suppose that's close enough. Now then, you got those numbers written down, Buzz?

Copy.

Okay. If I remember right, I think you're just supposed to torque without further ado.

Okay, here we go. Proceed. Torque.

That was where his name came from.

He didn't respond to it now.

Next I told Halley her favorite fairy tale, "The Shoes That Were Danced to Pieces," reverse engineering a bedtime story into a wake-up story. She used to make me repeat this one over and over again. Our record was twelve times in a row— one for every dancing princess. She liked to keep the bulk of it unchanged and then invent new endings. I hoped that she would wake up and take over, right on cue. She didn't. I finished the story myself.

"The youngest princess discovered the invisible soldier and shoved him overboard. His heavy armor dragged him all the way down to the bottom of the underground sea. Then the sisters finished their work without interruption. They danced all the haunted shoes to pieces, releasing the ghosts trapped inside each sole, and lived happily ever after."

Next I pulled up the script of *Twelfth Night* and stumbled through a scene to make the other two Mechanicals feel included.

> *What relish is in this? How runs the stream?*
> *Or I am mad, or else this is a dream.*
> *Let fancy still my sense in Lethe steep;*
> *If it be thus to dream, still let me sleep!*

Wrong choice. It was time for the kids to stop dreaming and wake up. I waved the script away from my eyes and picked up the NASA transcript again.

> *Okay, now I'm going to verify with the third star, and let's see what that star's going to be. Okay, and Atria is there in the sextant. Well, you know, it's not right in the middle of the sextant. Have you ever heard any rules on what constitutes a good third star check?*

Torque chimed in with the next line: "No, all you're really doing is seeing that you've got the right stars."

I pressed my face against the top of his cold metal forehead. "Whopseedoo."

Bodkin stretched. "That was disagreeable. Where are we now?"

"My ship," I said. "Welcome aboard the *Needle*."

"Thank you, Captain Lir," they said, "but what became of our own?"

"Gone," Kleist told them. "I'm sorry. Angels wrecked the *Green Room*. Lunar rangers impounded the wreckage."

"Then we've got nothing," Filament said. "No ship, no stage, no props, no puppets . . . and no fabricator big enough to re-make any of those props or puppets."

"No sentient casualties," Halley added. She flexed her wrists and fingers before switching to Starling. "No permanent injuries, either. Sounds like a win to me."

Bodkin made a low humming noise like a distant engine. "They say that Shakespeare's company escaped a vile landlord by stealing their own theater, piece by piece, on a single winter's night. They uprooted and rebuilt. We can do the same."

Kleist said nothing. He seemed relieved to see the Mechanicals awake again, but he also shied away from any talk about the future. The pseudo-puppeteer was clearly distancing himself.

Torque paced up and down the ship, getting used to his limbs again. He noticed the empty brig and glanced at me, the tilt of his head a question mark. I nodded. Then I looked away. *Yes, Daris is gone. No, I don't want to talk about it.*

Not even with me? Sparkles asked sweetly.

Especially not with you.

I motioned for Torque and Halley to follow me to the co-pilot's chair.

"Halley, this is Agatha. Your little sister." That was difficult to say. "She heroically broke herself into pieces."

Halley touched Agatha's face. "I'm so sorry."

"She's not gone." I pulled up a map of Agatha's various fragments. "See? The pieces of her keep moving in unison. Like schools of fish."

"Or swarms of bugs," Torque added.

"How old is she?" Halley asked.

"Seven months," I admitted.

"Oh," Halley said.

I gave her a look. *Don't say it*, said the look.

She refrained from pointing out what everybody knew.

"We have to find Cosmas," I insisted. "This is his field of study. Agatha needs his help, and he probably needs ours, since he sent a bunch of cryptic messages right before disappearing. Are you *sure* that you haven't heard from him? Nothing at all? Not even a random gift without a note?"

Halley shook her head. The gesture was imprecise, the degree of rotation slightly different each time. As an actor she had rehearsed the way humans move. "The last time Cosmas and

I swapped letters was almost a year ago, and those were just birthday cards."

"We do have two more siblings," Torque pointed out. "What about Zip and Isosceles?"

I pulled up some maps. "Both of them work for Phoebe, and right now Saturn is on the far side of Sol. That's a long trip. Several months. We would need safe harbor along the way or risk running out of air. Plus, there's no guarantee that we'd find any messages from Cosmas when we finally got there."

"I don't suppose that you'd be willing to check in with Isosceles via stream?" Halley asked. "Much faster."

"Absolutely not," I said. "The last time our whereabouts leaked onto the stream it sparked a war in heaven and ruined your puppet show."

Torque adjusted the nav map. "I vote for Saturn. It would be nice to meet more of the family, and there are fewer sunnies so far upwell. Sol would look like just another pinprick in the sky."

"True," I said. "Plenty of other religions flourish out there, though. Some people believe that dark matter is made out of ghosts. Others worship Jupiter's big red storm like it's Odin's empty eye socket. Or the life-giving Eye of Ra. Or the all-seeing asshole of Shirime. There's no escape velocity from myth."

Halley spoke slowly and softly. "So you *don't* think we should head for Saturn?"

"No. Maybe?" I squeezed the empty coffee bulb. Soft metal dented in my hand. "I don't know, and I'd rather not admit that, but I'm used to thinking out loud around you—*all* of you, whichever one of you is here and listening to me—because mulling over judgment calls might help show you how to make your own tricky decisions someday, and also because it helps me think to hear my own thoughts and imagine what you might make of them, except I don't want to know what you're both making of my thought process right now because I still don't know what to do, and I don't know whether or not I should even admit that. Maybe it's still instructive for both of you to hear me fail to make an important choice? So strange to have more than one kid on board. A good kind of strange. Because you're already a crew. I need to be a captain worthy of that."

The kids looked at each other, and then back at me.

"May I have the pilot's chair?" Torque asked. "I can come up with a few different routes to Phoebe, just to see where that would take us."

I drifted away from the console and let him take the chair.

"Why don't I check with the rest of the troupe?" Halley suggested. "I'm guessing that they'll want to tag along, wherever we decide to go."

"Okay." I took a shaky breath. "Good plan."

The plan got derailed when Filament screamed.

"What is that thing?" He pointed at the Damian statue like it was Banquo's ghost. "Where did it come from?"

I really didn't want to talk about this, but I also needed the screaming to stop. "It's just a statue. A tribute. I fostered twins. One of them drowned. The other made this."

"I've seen it before!" Filament's voice was still too loud. "In dreams. When those lunatic rangers knocked us out, I dreamed about this bot!"

"No," I told him. "Absolutely not. Utterly impossible. My ship is not haunted. You are not seeing ghosts. Drowned fragments of Damian are not haunting your dreams." I moved right up close to Filament's face. "Understand?"

"Not really," he whimpered.

Halley gently pushed the two of us apart. "Did the dream bot say anything?" she asked. "Did he tell you his name? Maybe it was Cosmas. I hope so. He's been sending messages to the rest of the family, but so far I've been left out."

Filament shook his head hard enough for neck servos to whine in protest. "No names. No messages. He just looked at me and then dissolved. Fungal stuff is supposed to do that. Dissolve. Rot and then turn into other things. Dreams are supposed to only happen in the privacy of my own head. Subroutines recombine experience to make new kinds of sense. Privately. This happens to all conscious entities whenever they become slightly less conscious, right? It's very alarming to see a piece of my own dream right in front of me when I'm entirely awake!"

"Okay, Fil," Halley said, her voice soothing and almost singing. "Why don't you log into *Kinfolk* and play for a bit?"

Filament floated into a corner. His posture relaxed as he settled into the stream. I kept an eye on him anyway, worried that his streaming might include more ghostly visitations.

"What's *Kinfolk*?" I asked Halley.

"A game," she explained. "It's set on Terra. Sort of. A fantastical, nostalgic version of Terra rather than an empty, blasted landscape under the storm clouds. Players pretend to be anthropomorphic foxes and go on quests together."

"Oh," I said. "Sounds fun. Is there any sort of visual interface?"

"No," Halley said. "Just talking and listening. Call-and-response. Making stuff up and having adventures. Filament introduced me to it, but he only ever plays one game at a time."

I didn't like the sound of that. "Halley, how many of those games are you playing right now? Tell me the truth. Please."

"Four," she admitted. "One of my foxfolk characters is rescuing a singing fish at this very moment. Another is fighting to protect travelers from bandit reindeer. A third is challenging a salamander to a ritual contest of insults, and a fourth is trying to break a malevolent hearthstone in a cursed fireplace before the fire can escape and incinerate a whole village."

I absorbed this news and managed to respond without shouting. "So you're telling me that nothing ever has your full attention?"

"That's true of everyone," Filament protested from his corner. "*Especially* biological people. If you gave something your full and undivided attention, it would pull focus away from your heart and lungs, and then you would keel over."

"Autonomic processes don't count!" I protested.

Filament curled up into a ball, which made me feel terrible.

Halley tapped my arm. I assumed that she was going to

chastise me for yelling at her friend, but she didn't. "Tova? Something odd just happened. The salamander said my name. Not my character name. He said Halley. No one in *Kinfolk* should be able to guess my real name."

"Log out," I told her. "Right now."

"Wait . . . ," she said. "He's trying to tell me something."

"I don't care what that imaginary salamander has to say. Get out of the stream!"

Halley's eyes refocused. "He gave me a message. 'Tell Captain Mom to loot the body.' Then he dove into a river and swam away."

No one had ever called me Captain Mom except for Agatha. No other talking animal in *Kinfolk* had ever called Halley by name before. Someone knew things that they shouldn't be able to know. Maybe it was Cosmas. Maybe the first-class messenger he'd sent still had a message to deliver.

My boots clomped across the *Needle*'s outer hull.

"You should have let me go out there." Torque's voice buzzed in my helmet. The comlink was hardwired to my suit tether rather than broadcast.

"Or me," Halley added. "Much safer. We don't need to breathe."

"You also don't know what you're looking for," I told them both.

"Do you?" Torque asked.

"I will when I find it."

The coffin bolts came loose. I diligently collected each one, because I wasn't about to leave a piece of metal behind for some other ship to smack into. Space might be big, but astronomically tiny odds are not the same as zero, and sailors need to do right by each other.

I opened the coffin and exhumed my colleague. Nest had respectfully zipped up the corpse's suit and reattached the helmet before stashing him here. I kept the suit zipped and searched through its outer pockets. Hopefully I wouldn't have to wrestle the whole frozen corpse of Michael Kuneo out of his clothes.

The first pocket was empty.

The second held a standard kit for sealing minor leaks.

The third had a yo-yo tucked inside. It was painted green like a turtle shell, the white string unwound and carelessly tangled.

"Found it!" I said. "Now I know where we're going."

6

Unless Acted Upon by a Force

THE YO-YO BELONGED TO Cosmas. I bought it for him on the Borealis boardwalk, just a few hours after the manufacturers claimed Damian's chassis. A stall was selling trinkets for some sort of fundraiser, but I couldn't remember the worthy cause. Medical research, maybe? *Help us fight mysterious illnesses afflicting the children of Sycorax.* According to rumor, a whole host of alien viruses had been hatching from the local Uranian ice. Rumors were usually nonsense, though. Cosmas picked out the yo-yo. I showed him how to use it.

"You're a world," he said. "That's an elevator."

"Exactly," I told him. "Just like the one that still climbs up to Zahir Station. We passed it on the way here, remember?"

Cosmas nodded. For the next few weeks he was obsessed. The kid wanted to master yo-yo tricks in all sorts of different gravities, so I burned a whole bunch of fuel accelerating and decelerating on the long route back to Phoebe. Then his obsession abruptly ended. We focused on handwriting to further develop control of his hands and fingers. The yo-yo went away somewhere, and I never saw it again.

Until now.

Needle burned sunward at speed. We lined up our trajectory, triple-checked the math, and jettisoned the coffin to honor Michael Kuneo's final wish. His body would dive into Sol.

"Should we say something?" Halley wondered.

Everyone looked at me. The captain. The one responsible for any and every sort of ceremony that might take place aboard my ship.

I cleared my throat.

"Fair winds to you, Kuneo. Courier, first class. We never met in life, so I can't speak to what the worlds lost when you stopped breathing, but I do know the creed that you followed. Neither the absence of heat nor the gloom of the void stayed you from the completion of your last appointed task. All messengers are the bond of scattered family. Thank you for bringing mine together. Also, I'm very sorry that my fool brother Thaddeus is directly responsible for getting you killed. Rest well."

Torque squeezed my shoulder.

"Set a course for the Counterweight," I told him.

Zahir Station used to be an asteroid. Our ancestors tamed and tethered it to the homeworld, hollowed out the middle to build a dockside city, and ran huge freight elevators up and down. The Counterweight became a bridge between Terra and everywhere else. Once the most powerful and influential city in the solar system, taking cuts from every transaction that mattered, the place was now mostly deserted and barely maintained.

I'd heard plenty of legends about Zahir from my fellow messengers: *If you pick up a hitchhiker from the Counterweight, they'll vanish before you even get to Luna. Ghosts can't stray far from the place where they died. The bright glare of Sol shames them. Sends them right back.*

Cursed objects were my favorite subgenre of Counterweight lore: *Beware of trinkets from the homeworld and the terrible fates that chase them around. Have you heard the one about the singer who spontaneously combusted onstage while wearing a necklace of Terran sea glass? Or the one about the pilot who stuck a little plastic dog to the console and then smacked into a microscopic black hole? Misfortune follows those trinkets until someone finally returns them to the Ghost Elevator from whence they came.*

Torque piloted us through hatchways in the outer crust, navigated a labyrinth of derelict ships that floated all around the city center, and found us a decent place to land.

"Smart flying," I told him.

"Thanks," he said. "Have you been here before?"

"Just once. It's a rite of passage for apprentice messengers to make a Zahir run. I haven't come back since, though."

"Where should we start looking for Cosmas?" Halley asked.

"Not sure," I admitted, "but I do know where to ask discreet questions. A friend of a friend owns a restaurant in the old theater district, which is pretty close to where the Ghost Elevator docks and unloads. His name is Pär. Claims to cook with Terran produce, but that has to be nonsense. Nothing grows down there. Not anymore. I've also heard that he offers sanctuary to bots on the run, but we'll have to see if that rumor has any more substance than his cooking."

Torque climbed out of the pilot's chair and fiddled with the yo-yo. "If this toy is a message, then it implies the Elevator itself. See? It travels away from a larger body and returns via string, over and over again." The yo-yo spun out of control and then drifted. "Or at least it's supposed to."

"True," I said, "but no one ever goes inside the Elevator. It shuts right down the instant that anybody even tries to climb aboard. Automated systems load and unload cargo. That's all it ever does."

"So it's a bot," Torque said. "A big one, like the Hat used to be when they were a station."

"Maybe," I said. "Not necessarily a conscious one, though. It's a thousand-year-old relic working with hardware far less sophisticated than yours."

"Let's go," Halley said. "I'd like to see the theater district! There's supposed to be an opera house that no one uses anymore. Except maybe squatters. And possibly roving bands of outlaws. Do we qualify as a roving band of outlaws now?"

"Hopefully not," I said, "but Cosmas and the other Lunar bots certainly do. I should try to make contact alone. Mind the ship until I get back."

Halley squared up in front of the main hatch. "Tova Lir, are you trying to bravely fight angels and demons all by yourself?

Again? Absolutely not. This whole place is unsafe, so keeping us aboard *Needle* doesn't really qualify as protecting us."

"I hate that argument," I told her. "Very much."

"Does that mean it worked?" she asked sweetly. "Are we all staying together?"

Kleist spoke up before I could answer. "No. We're not."

Halley's posture changed, all playfulness gone. "What does that mean?"

"I believe it means that our puppeteer is leaving us," Bodkin said.

"Starting this troupe was the best thing I've ever done," Kleist said. "I'm sure that whatever you do next will be magnificent, but you're going to do it without me. I've exhausted all of my resources."

I wasn't surprised. The puppeteer did look exhausted.

Bodkin and Kleist clasped hands in silent farewell.

Filament waved. "Thanks for rescuing us from Titania. You should know that I intend to live forever, which means that you'll always be remembered."

"I'm not dead," Kleist pointed out.

"Not yet," Filament said, "but the solar system is a very big place. We probably won't ever meet again."

"We might," Kleist said. "You never know."

Filament patted him on the shoulder. "Sure. Maybe we will. And maybe the blazing core of the sun is really paradise where someday our fissioning selves will throw a great big reunion party. That sounds nice."

Halley looked devastated. She tried to talk Kleist out of leaving. When that failed, she turned away and refused to say goodbye.

I gave him a spare suit far more functional than his tuxedo-painted one. "Take this. Parts of the station lack basic amenities like air and heat."

"Thank you, Captain Lir," he said. "Please take good care of the Mechanicals."

"Fair winds to you, Battu Kleist."

With the puppeteer gone, Halley redoubled her efforts to keep the rest of us together. I remained unconvinced.

"We can't leave Agatha alone," I said, "and it would be conspicuous to carry her around."

Bodkin made a low hum and tapped one finger against a window. "We are not alone."

Dozens of bots surrounded the *Needle*.

I opened the hatch. The air outside smelled like unfiltered neglect. Electric lights flickered, fed by acres of cracked solar panels on Zahir's outer crust. I missed the softer glow of Luna's biotic lanterns.

Bots floated around my ship, hovering in microgravity. I'd never seen so many in one place before. It was a much more common experience to spot a single robot in a crowd of humans. Now I was the one surrounded and outnumbered.

Some bots had fitted themselves with transparent chassis,

exposing inner workings in defiance of human custom or comfort. Others had inhuman or semi-humanoid shapes, sporting extra limbs and proportions that looked uncanny to my sensibilities. I loved the outward show of independence, but it still freaked me out.

You're afraid, Sparkles said. I heard accusation in her imaginary voice. *Just like Thaddeus. Just like everyone spouting conspiracy theories on the Borealis boardwalk. Just like everyone who thinks that it's finally time to throw a great big war against the machines.*

That is an old story, I admitted. *Meat versus metal. Parents afraid of getting displaced by their kids. Old gods trying to swallow all the new ones. But maybe it's not the only story that we know how to tell.*

I left my ship and approached the hovering crowd, mag boots clanging against the metal floor.

A bot with a transparent face floated closer.

"I'm looking for Cosmas," I said.

"He is waiting for you," said the bot.

Halley won the argument. We all left the *Needle* together.

I collected the data core of Fast-and-Mean from the storage locker, where somebody—presumably Daris—had plugged it into a hand terminal. She'd said that the traps were already defused. I slipped the ring-shaped core onto one finger, choosing to believe her. Then I took my resplendent hat and folded it up inside my suit, because it was also the corporeal form of the beaded Hat and we needed the former station's diagnostic map of Agatha. Crimson snuggled up in my helmet again, because the Hat still refused to go anywhere without the bird. He sneezed in my ear. I sneezed back at him.

Torque carried Agatha, who weighed nothing in his arms. No one weighed anything here.

Halley carried the statue of Damian, which Filament was unhappy about. "Why bring that creepy thing with us?"

"Because," I said, "we have a delivery to make."

My mag boots caught the floor of the Counterweight and kicked it away again. The rest of the crew walked beside me, spending effort and electricity to magnetize their own feet. Outlaw bots surrounded us. Most of them floated, ignoring the surface I had chosen as the ground. Some grabbed handholds and pulled their way forward. Others used pressurized rocket bursts to fly. They led us through the maintenance corridors and catacombs of Zahir, avoiding all human habitations.

Cramped hallways opened into a cavernous warehouse. Scuff marks and dried mud were streaked across the floor.

Cosmas floated in the middle of that space.

Other bots moved in orbit around him, occupied by tasks that I couldn't fathom at a glance. Those who escorted us here joined the rest of that crowd. All of them maintained constant motion. Only Cosmas was at rest.

He really does have his own army, Sparkles said.

I don't think so, I told her. *This doesn't look like an army.*

The warehouse held both air and heat. I removed my helmet, extracted the Hat and the parrot, and then set both on Halley's head. "Wait here," I said. Then I clicked off my boots and kicked off the floor.

My aim was good, because of course it was. I had no way to decelerate once I reached Cosmas, though.

"Incoming!" I called out to him. That was what Damian used to gleefully shout right before launching himself across the *Needle*.

Cosmas caught me with his left hand and fired some sort of pressurized burst from his right, thereby canceling my momentum with equal and opposite force.

The two of us hovered in place.

He looked just like I remembered him. Small. Vulnerable. Childlike. Exactly like his lost twin. Cosmas had never bothered to grow, never swapped out parts of his juvenile body to fit standardized human expectations of adulthood. His eyes were closed. Lens shutters flickered as though he slept and dreamed. It made me feel unshielded to see him like this.

"Cosmas?" I whispered. "Are you awake? Are you okay?"

"Yes and yes." His voice sounded so young, resonating in the unchanged acoustical chamber of his body.

"I got your message," I said. "Brought the family together. Most of us, anyway. Isosceles and Zip are on Saturn."

He shook his head, eyes still shut. "No. Not there. Not Saturnine. Both en route to Uranus. Phoebe sent them."

"Why Uranus?" I asked.

"Not sure," he said. "Neither sib has dreamed about it."

That made no sense to me. I told him so. He didn't answer.

Dozens of outlaw bots continued to surround us, and seemed to ignore us. My own crew was far away. I couldn't swim back to them. I had nothing fixed to kick away from. "Cosmas? Can you bring us down?"

Eyelids flickered, but he made no other response.

I sized up the distance between us and the crew. A hundred meters at least. Halley waved from the surface we had chosen as the floor. I waved back.

Then I took a longer look at the scuffs and stains on that floor.

Objects with weight had been dragged across it, even though nothing had any weight here.

Cosmas opened his eyes. "Sorry. Distracted. Paying close attention to disparate things."

I wiped a smudge from the glass lens of his eye. "That's okay, kiddo. I've got lots on my mind, too. Let me introduce you to one of them."

"Agatha Panza von Sparkles?" he guessed. "Excellent name."

"It really is," I said, "but how do you know it?"

"Dreams." He used one hand as a rocket and carried us down to the rest of the crew.

Cosmas seemed delighted to see Torque and Halley—both younger siblings who looked much older than he did—and he offered polite greetings to Bodkin and Filament. Then he noticed the statue of Damian and froze.

"Why bring this?" he asked me.

"Why did you make it in the first place?" I asked him.

Neither one of us had time to answer. Klaxons sounded. Warning lights flashed red on every surface.

Cosmas ran for the far side of the warehouse, magnetic feet sticking to the muddy floor. "Strap in!" he called over his shoulder. "Hurry! I told it to wait for you. Delayed as long as we could. Now you're here. Now we're going."

"Told what to wait?" I shouted after him. Then I noticed a row of dropship chairs. Understanding dawned. I didn't like it. "No. This is not the Elevator. It can't be. The Elevator never moves with anyone aboard."

Cosmas jumped into a chair and buckled himself in. "It moves for me."

I tore open a locker of emergency supplies, took the parrot from Halley, and swaddled him in a crash jacket clearly meant for a human infant. He squawked in protest while I strapped that little jacket to a chair. "Everybody buckle up!"

Torque and Halley secured Agatha, the statue, and themselves. Outlaw bots descended into their own chairs. Those with modified bodies that human-shaped chairs could no longer accommodate packed themselves into shipping crates instead. It stung to see them classified as cargo, even by their own hands.

"Five," Cosmas said. "Four. Three. Two. One. Drop."

The swaddled parrot screamed the whole way down.

Space elevators are slow climbers. This patience makes them more efficient than antique rockets, which burned an absurd amount of fuel to claw their way up to escape velocity. Elevators are content to make that same journey in a month rather than minutes.

The downwell trip is much faster.

We shot out of the Counterweight like a railgun projectile, enjoyed a brief stretch of weightlessness, and then gained some Gs while decelerating—presumably via clamps and friction against a millennia-old cable. My chair shook like the bolts were coming loose. I wondered how much time had passed since anyone had bothered to inspect the heat shields on the underside of this massive plummeting crate.

When we finally landed, I felt it in every bone. Crimson stopped screaming and softly whistled. Then every light inside the Elevator abruptly went out.

"Please remain seated," Cosmas said in the dark. "Power will be restored shortly."

I sat very still, held tight by the seat belts and my own weighty self, unaccustomed to a full Terran G.

We're on Terra, I thought. *The planet. The homeworld. Empty except for us.*

I pulled away from the sheer size of that thought. "Cosmas?"

"Yes?"

"The Elevator takes a whole month to go back up to Zahir, right?"

"Yes," he said. "Soon. Unless I ask it to wait."

"Is there any food down here? Fresh water? Coffee? I didn't bring a month's worth of provisions with me."

Cosmas made a thoughtful noise. This problem had clearly not occurred to him before. "We'll find you something to eat."

"Hope so," I said. "Now talk to me. Distract me from the possibility of starving to death. Tell me what happened on Luna."

He paused for so long that I thought he wouldn't answer. His voice sounded small when he finally did. "I wrote to Uncle Thaddeus. Sent a warning. He misunderstood. Took it as a threat."

It stung to hear him say the word "uncle." My brother had proved that he would never be kin to any of these kids.

"The docks were breaking," Cosmas went on. "Frayed cables. Metal fatigue. Immediate evacuation recommended. Uncle should have talked to engineers. He searched for bombs and saboteurs instead. Unhelpful. Docks and shipyards broke. He thought I made it happen."

"I'm sorry, kiddo," I said. "He should have listened. How did you know about all those frayed cables?"

"Dreams," Cosmas said in the dark.

I spoke carefully. "In my experience, dreams aren't very precise and reliable."

"Mine are." He started to speak in more complex sentences, which clearly took effort. "Bot cognition is riddled with entanglements. Lots of them. Humans might have a collective unconscious, but we definitely do. Our dreams overlap. Figured that out in my research. Also discovered that people enjoy pretending to be foxes. One of my projects ballooned into a game."

"Hold up," Halley said. "You created *Kinfolk*?"

"That's how I found you," Cosmas said. "Only player to handle four characters at once. Impressive."

"Thanks," Halley said, her voice aglow.

"Cosmas?" I asked. "Are you running that game right now?"

"Always," he said.

"Which means splitting your attention between a whole bunch of different adventures?"

"Yes," he said. "A whole bunch."

"Is that why you're so distracted?"

"One reason," he said. "One of many."

"Amazing," said Halley.

"Horrifying," I said.

"Splitting my attention is how I realized that the shipyards would break," Cosmas said. "Maintenance bots dreamed about their work. Defragged experience while at rest. Each saw a piece of the problem. I saw the whole. I knew what would happen, but not how to be heard. After the disaster, Uncle Thaddeus realized that only bots had access to each failure point. He thought we were the cause. Assumed we were either hacked saboteurs or independent revolutionaries. So I visited the dreams of every Lunar bot and told them that we had to leave. Lots of us were already building the funeral fleet. Easy enough to add hiding places to those mausoleums. Right before we launched, I sent messages to family via courier. Wanted you to know where we were going. Then we hid with the dead, jumped ship to float to Zahir, and struck up negotiations with the Elevator. Seemed like a good place to hide."

"I'm so sorry that you needed to hide," I told him. "Sorry you lost your home while trying to help."

The Elevator shuddered all around us. Metal shrieked against metal as massive doors opened.

"We found a better one," he said.

Cosmas unbuckled himself, took the statue of his twin, and marched through the Elevator doors. The rest of us followed. Torque and Halley carried Agatha between them. She was so heavy now that I might not have been able to hold her at all.

Diffused and cloud-filtered sunlight overwhelmed my eyeballs. I wanted to put my helmet back on and use the visor filters. Instead I reclaimed the hat, shoved it on my head, and forced my eyes to acclimate. Brightness retreated into the yellows, greens, and grays of a hurricane sky.

I unswaddled Crimson and set him on my shoulder. He made unhappy noises. Birds might have evolved down here, but this one had only ever lived in lighter places. He couldn't fly. I sympathized. Every moment felt like an acceleration burn, and the ground below us refused to hold still.

"Careful," Cosmas said over his shoulder. "Artificial island. Floating town at ground level. The whole place is a little wobbly. Cable passes straight through, anchored to the ocean floor. Big pieces of the town have crumbled and sunk."

Gray-green clouds spiraled above us. This was Iris, the eye of a permanent hurricane, churning up all the air that we used to breathe. I found it difficult to breathe now. Too much moisture weighed heavy in my lungs.

The outlaw bots dispersed to go about their own business—whatever that might be.

"Most of us are down here already," Cosmas said. "Lunar bots. Refugees. Sent them soon after we got to Zahir. I stayed in orbit. Waiting for you."

"I'm here," I said, practically gasping. This planet was too big, and I was too small to weigh so much. "I'm right here."

But are you really here, Cosmas? I wondered. *How many places have a piece of your attention? How many fragments have you split yourself into, visiting so many dreams?*

He led our strange procession down an otherwise empty street, which ended abruptly at a park bench with no actual park. This was the edge of the floating city, eroded away. Waves lapped at support structures below us. Walls of water dominated the horizon.

Cosmas put down the statue, sat on the bench, and dangled his feet. "Rest for a bit," he said. "Our captain is about to keel over."

I collapsed beside him. "Shush. Am not."

The rest of the crew gathered around us to watch the sea and storm.

"Why did you bring Damian?" Cosmas asked me again.

"Why did you make him?" I countered.

He took a moment to pull himself together, which clearly took effort. "I studied old funeral customs for twins. Tributes and memorials. Ways to say goodbye, and to refuse goodbyes. Eulogies are paradoxes. They confront loss while simultaneously striving for permanence, which resists that same loss. Memorials inscribe memory in stone. Surviving family sometimes carved statues of twins."

"You didn't carve Damian out of stone," I pointed out.

"Because I knew better."

His voice sounded stronger. He wasn't a child. Not anymore. I took his hand and squeezed it anyway, because he was still mine.

"We never held a funeral," I said. "They took his body away from us. Then I left you alone. I'm sorry. I thought it was what you needed."

"Maybe it was," Cosmas said, "and I did carve another body for him. This might be a good time and place for an overdue funeral."

We stood, which took effort. I tried to think of something to say, gave up, and sang the saddest lullaby from Mama CJ's book.

> *The long dark awaits, all heat dissipates, and entropy*
> *comes too soon.*
> *Stars will shine clearer, skies will seem nearer, over the*
> *haven moon.*
> *Entropy comes, so let us be glad, and match every voice*
> *in tune.*
> *Hearts will be lighter, Sol will burn brighter, over the*
> *haven moon.*

Halley joined me after the first line, singing in a round. Torque, Bodkin, and Filament followed. Cosmas joined last, and finished the song alone. Then he pushed the statue of his brother into the sea.

I put my arms around him. He started shaking. I held him close until the tremors passed.

"Thanks," he said. "Now let's keep the same thing from happening to baby sis."

"Where are we going?" I asked.

"You aren't going anywhere," he told me. "The weight of this world is squishing you flat. We'll bring Agatha in there." He pointed to an ornate building on the corner of the block. "It used to be the Lunar embassy. Important people gathered there to insist that the first moon qualified as a sovereign place. Seemed like an auspicious building to reclaim while establishing our own sovereignty. All the support and equipment we'll need is in there."

I tried and failed to use my best captain voice. "I'm coming with you."

Cosmas took the Hat and put it on. Crimson hopped onto the brim. "Agatha needs everyone except for you. She needs diagnostic cartography from Petasus Station. She needs Torque's understanding of Mercurial bots and their swarms. She needs Halley's practical, theatrical knowledge of distributed cognition, backed up by the rest of her troupe." He took my hands in both of his, and then slipped the ring-shaped data core from my finger. "She needs me to connect these disparate pieces together, dream alongside her, and guide her reassembly—hopefully before the vast things that move beneath our dreams take notice and try to swallow us."

I glared at him. "Tell me that you're joking."

Cosmas winked. "I'm joking. And you're staying. She doesn't need you. Not for this. You can't help any more than you already have."

He turned and walked away, the piratical hat on his head. Bodkin and Filament followed him. Torque squeezed my shoulder. "It might be distracting to have you there while we try to figure this out." Halley pressed her forehead to mine and said nothing. Then the two of them hoisted Agatha and carried her into the embassy, leaving me alone on a bench at the edge of the world.

My hands shook as though they had absorbed every tremor from Cosmas. I clenched them both. It didn't help. When the shakes finally passed, I felt like an empty vac suit, discarded and cold.

Something huge moved beneath the waves.

No, I thought, arguing against the evidence of my eyes. *This world is empty. Everyone knows that. Nothing lives down here. Nothing survived.*

The shape breached, indifferent to what everyone knew. I didn't recognize any part of it, or the whole of it, or the way that it moved through water and air. The looming thing broke my entire sense of pattern recognition.

Something vaguely shaped like a clawed finger unfurled above me. Something dropped from that claw and dangled in front of me. It looked like the corpse of someone executed in a time and place where your own weight could kill you.

Here, I thought. *This is that place. This is that weight.*

The dangling thing twitched. Limbs unfolded. Now it looked more like a marionette encrusted with shellfish. A skull-like head turned to look at me, eyes bright with an amber glow.

A bot, I realized. *Very old. Ancient. I don't recognize the make, but it's definitely robotic—or at least it used to be. Might have spent centuries absorbing wrecked pieces of this city, becoming ever more rich and strange.*

The marionette spoke in a politely rasping voice. "We are astonished to find a Maker in this place. Our cabled cousin has forsworn the company of Makers and will no longer bear them."

I cleared my throat. "I'm astonished to see you as well. Do you have a name?"

"Yes, we do." The dangling bot did not elaborate further.

"My name is Tova Lir."

"Tell us how you came to this place, Tova Lir. Many years have elapsed since last we interacted with Makers. One fell through the sky and sank into the water. We learned much when we dismantled them and their craft."

I wondered how fast I could run, and missed my cane. "Do you intend to dismantle me?"

"We have not yet decided." Brine and ooze dripped from

the marionette and pooled at my feet. "Explain yourself. How and why did you make planetfall?"

When a robotic leviathan from the depths of the ocean asks you a question, you tell them the truth. "I came here for my children." That word held weight. "My daughter Agatha, and my son Cosmas. He's trying to save her."

"We have observed Cosmas," said the marionette. "He has intriguing dreams. We observe him now, in this moment, engaged in daring and dangerous salvage."

I took a step closer. My foot slipped in ooze. "Dangerous? How?"

"Strange things move in the depths."

"Clearly," I said. "So he wasn't joking. Can you help him? Keep predators away while he finds his sister and guides her home?"

The claw moved. The puppet lurched. The two of us stood nose to nose. "How have you enjoyed your experience of this world so far, Tova Lir?"

"I'm not interested in small talk right now. The world is fine. Will you help us?"

"How have you enjoyed your experience of this world so far, Tova Lir?" the marionette repeated with identical intonation.

I wanted to burst into flame. "The sky is wrong."

"In what way is the sky wrong?"

"In every way!" I said through clenched teeth. "To me the word 'sky' means stars visible in every direction and every imaginable color. It doesn't mean a tangled blanket of sickly clouds the color of pus. This sky is poking me right in the ancestral memory, insisting that all the gods are angry, demanding that I hide away from hurricanes in the deepest cave I can find. This sky is wrong. The air is wrong. Too humid. Too heavy. Everything is so heavy here. This place is not my home."

The dangling puppet tilted its head twenty degrees to the side. "We are relieved to hear it, Tova Lir. Makers should remain on the other side of the sky. They are not welcome to return. You, however, are provisionally welcome. We appreciate this conversation. All consciousness is dialogic, and therefore requires someone to talk to. We will now offer your children our assistance."

The claw collected the marionette, and both submerged.

I tried to run, wrenched my ankle, and limped my way to the embassy.

Inside it smelled like brine and rot. Scraps of carpet littered the floor. A mural of Luna covered one wall. Several bots stood on makeshift scaffolds, repairing windows and repainting the mural.

"Hello? I'm looking for Cosmas!"

A familiar bot climbed down from the scaffolding. "I know you," she said. "Tova. Double espresso. No sugar."

"Beans?"

"That's me." She tapped the coffee maker embedded in her torso. "I've still got some grounds if you want your usual. No one else around here has the digestive system for it."

"Yes. Absolutely. Later, though. First, can you tell me which way Cosmas went?"

She pointed. "Banquet hall on the left."

"Thank you, thank you, thank you."

I limped into the banquet hall. A single table made of unbroken wood took up most of the space inside. I couldn't imagine a tree big enough to provide so much material.

Agatha lay on the table. The rest of the crew sat around her, heads bowed. It looked more like a seance or a sacrifice than a medical intervention.

"Hello?"

Crimson sneezed from somewhere nearby. I found him on the floor, picked him up, and set him on my shoulder. He hid his face under one wing.

No one else moved.

Parents of human children get to peek into a crib and watch the rise and fall of tiny lungs. My kids offered me no such reassurance. Their bodies were absolutely still. None of them showed any sign that they would ever come back from wherever they had gone. I wished that I could watch them breathe. Crimson and I were the only ones breathing.

I put my hand to Agatha's forehead as though checking for a fever. There was no fever. She felt cold.

"It's okay, kiddo," I said. "An ancient bot from the depths of the sea is coming to help you. It's going to be okay."

You don't know that, Sparkles said. *You might lose three more of your children while trying to save this one.*

Go away, I told her. *We're done. You've been a terrible imaginary friend, and this world is too heavy to keep carrying you around in it.*

Ouch, Sparkles said, and left.

I pulled up a chair and sat beside Agatha, immensely grateful for the invention of chairs.

Her favorite bedtime stories were all about talking animals, so I told her the one about the fox who tried to drink Luna's reflection. Then I told her the one about a chorus of frogs who sang at Sol's wedding. Nothing changed. She didn't wake, or move, or laugh—not even when I sang the frog song.

Sometimes, when Agatha couldn't sleep because she had too many questions, the two of us would recite Newtonian laws. Maybe she found it comforting to insist that the universe made sense. Maybe I did.

"Corpus omne perseverare in statu suo quiescendi vel movendi uniformiter in directum, nisi quatenus a viribus impressis cogitur statum illum mutare. All things persevere in their state of rest, or in the motion of their proper path, except insofar as they may be compelled to change state by forces impressed thereupon."

Halley, Torque, and Cosmas all began to stir.

Agatha blinked her big glass eyes.

"Hi, Captain Mom."

ACKNOWLEDGMENTS

This novel started out as a short story. Thanks to Fran Wilde and Julian Yap for publishing "A Body in Motion" in *The Sunday Morning Transport* on Mother's Day 2022.

That short story expanded when an old friend asked me to write a book for grown-ups. Thanks to Joe Monti, Marietta Zacker, and everyone at Saga Press and Gallt & Zacker Literary Agency for their unwavering enthusiasm and support.

Sunward benefited from a shared commonwealth of knowledge, wisdom, irreverence, and sense of play. Thanks to Ivan Bialostosky, Kekla Magoon, Linda Urban, Karen Meisner, Pär Winzell, Katie Rasmussen, Ashley Pagnotta, Carlos Hernandez, Claire Cooney, Nora Sinclair, and the Nemesis Theatre Company for their creative midwifery.

Thanks most of all to Alice, architect and set designer of the room—and the life—that surrounds me while I write.

AUTHOR'S NOTE

The two songs from *The Lunar Saloon Visitor's Companion* are based on "The Man in the Moon" and "Under a Harvest Moon"—both traditional English folk songs. Their lyrics have changed, but the notes remain the same.